DADDY'S LITTLE ONE

SCANDALOUS DADDIES BOOK 1

AJ ALEXANDER

Daddy's Little One
by AJ Alexander
www.authorajalexander.com
authorajalexander@gmail.com

Copyright © May 2022 by AJ Alexander
First E-book Publication: February 2020
Photo provided by: Despositphoto
Cover Designer: Cormar Covers
Editor: CPR Editing

CHAPTER ONE

JULIAN

"The first day of class is always the hardest. The students are antsy because all they've done is get drunk and party." Dr. Stephanie Francis prattles on as we enter the lecture hall.

This is old hat, nothing I don't already know, but she seems to be one of those eager-to-please types, so I indulge her.

"It's understandable. Break has ended and it's time to get serious." I drop my satchel on the podium.

"Julian, I doubt you'll have any issues. With your accent, you'll have them eating out of your hand." She places a hand on my arm and looks up at me through fluttering lashes.

I do my best to appease her, but she has no idea she isn't the woman I'm searching for. "Doesn't really matter as long as they turn in their assignments on time."

She gives my arm a gentle squeeze. "I'll leave you to get settled. If there's anything you need, my office is always open."

"I've got it covered from here. Thank you, Dr. Francis," I say with a smile before I unpack my bag.

The clicking of her heels on the floor signals her departure. Thank Christ for that. If I'd had to endure her flirting any longer, I would have booked a one-way ticket back home to merry old England.

I came to America for a temporary position at Danville University to teach Intro to Shakespeare. I didn't want to leave Cambridge, but the opportunity was too good to pass up for one very specific reason. *Meghan.*

I only meant my affair with Meghan to be temporary, a silly summer affair. I was mesmerized by her long blonde hair, eyes the color of the bluest ocean, a petite figure, and curves that would bring a man to his knees. My cock hardens when I think of the time we spent together.

We met by chance at a small café. She spilled a spot of scalding tea on my lap and somehow, we got along swimmingly. One thing led to another and the rest, as they say, was history.

"Oh, my God!" she exclaimed, covering her mouth with her hand. "I can't believe I did that. I'm so sorry."

My lap was on fire, and once it cooled, all I felt was wet. The woman who spilled the tea was frantically handing me tissue after tissue, taking them from nearby tables.

"I think I have things covered from here," I said, placing my hand over hers before it reached my cock.

"I'll pay to have them cleaned," she offered.

"It was a simple cock-up," I replied casually. "I was planning on purchasing another pair."

She digs into the leather bag slung across her body and pulls out a wad of pound notes. "Here. Let me pay for them."

I closed my hand over hers and smiled. "It's not a bother, truly. Why don't you have a seat?"

She obeys and lets out a heavy sigh. "I really am sorry. It's this jet lag. I know you're supposed to stay awake to let your body adjust, but honestly, I just want to take a nap."

I couldn't help my reaction to her innocence, to the sweetness radiating from her. She leaned forward, placed her elbows on the table, and rested her head in her hands. Her blonde hair was piled high on her head in a bun, and she wore a pair of olive-colored trousers and a floral blouse.

"Don't worry." Giving in to temptation, I reached out and put a hand on her knee. "No one will know if you take a nap during the middle of the day."

The memory of our first encounter brings a smile to my face. For some reason, I was able to keep her at my table, chatting happily, ignoring my soaking wet clothing. She was studying at Cambridge for the summer before returning home to her position as an adjunct professor at Danville. After our first kiss, I knew Meghan was special, that we'd last longer than the summer. When we parted ways, we promised to stay in touch. For a fortnight, we exchanged emails before all correspondence from her came to an abrupt stop.

As luck would have it, I got the call to be a guest lecturer in the English department a few weeks ago and jumped at the chance. Now I just have to find my girl.

My watch beeps, signaling it's time for my lecture to begin.

"It's now or never," I grumble into the empty lecture hall.

As if on cue, students file into the space. One by one, they take their seats, eagerly waiting for their college experience to begin.

"Everyone, take a seat quickly. We have a lot to cover today."

"Wait, you're actually teaching today?" a student asks.

"Your name?"

"Tyler."

I push my horn-rimmed glasses further up on my nose and level him with a practiced look. "Tyler, today is your first day of college. *Yes*, I plan on lecturing. You are here to learn, are you not?"

Crossing my arms over my chest, I wait for a response. Instead, Tyler mumbles under his breath as he takes a seat. As the trickle of students slows, I lean back against the podium and begin my introduction.

"My name is Julian. You can call me by my name; I'm not one for titles. This is Introduction to

Shakespeare." I turn toward the white board and write my contact information. "I will not have a teaching assistant for this class, so if you need help, contact me directly and I will try my best to assist you." I look over my shoulder as I continue writing. "If everyone would please examine their syllabus, we will go over it before we begin the lecture."

Papers and bags rustle as someone comes barging into the lecture hall.

"It is in your best interest to be on time for my class. In the future, the door will be locked once the lecture begins."

I do not address the latecomer. Tardiness is a pet peeve, and I won't indulge whoever is interrupting my attention.

"But I'm your new TA."

Two things make me turn at once. The familiar feminine voice, and that my intruder claims to be my teaching assistant. Anger boils in my veins. I'm astonished at the blatant disrespect for my wishes and the terms set forth in my contract by Stephanie and Danville University.

I spin on my heels and come face-to-face with the woman who has starred in my fantasies every night since she left my bed.

"Meghan?"

CHAPTER TWO

MEGHAN

This is both the worst and best day of my life.

Early this morning, I met with my advisor, Dr. Francis, who informed me I was still one class short of graduating.

"How is this even possible?" I wailed in her office. "I've taken every course required."

Dr. Francis shrugged. "I'm sorry, Meghan. Maybe some credits were lost when you transferred?"

"So, now what am I supposed to do? I already have a full course load this semester and I am *not* enrolling in summer school again."

This summer was magical, and I doubt I'll ever have another. Meeting Julian was the highlight of my trip to Cambridge, a trip that ultimately left me with nothing.

"I cannot believe you're leaving me in the morning," Julian whispered during our last night together. "I don't think I can bear to part with you."

His hold on me tightened, and I willingly sank deeper into the warmth and safety of his embrace.

"The new semester starts in a few months and now I've got to put all of this research together into a...thesis proposal.

Hopefully, my advisor accepts it," I answered, hoping he didn't catch my stumble.

I might have lied to Julian about my age...and my status at Danville University. At the time, I didn't think it was a big deal. Julian and I never talked about continuing our relationship, and honestly, I was quite happy with the distraction of a summer fling. But now that our time was ending, I wasn't ready to leave. Or to let him go.

He did things to my body I'd never experienced before. He made it sing for him.

I sat up slowly and let the straps of my black satin chemise fall from my shoulders. Julian's eyes darkened and he sucked in a breath.

"One more night," I whispered.

His eyes flicked up. "You know the magic word, little one."

"Daddy."

Back in the real world, Dr. Francis was talking, but I hardly listened.

"I have a solution." She sat straighter in her chair and folded her hands neatly on the desk in front of her. "We have a guest lecturer this semester. Dr. Armstrong has joined us from Cambridge. We normally assign these positions to grad students, but the position is yours if you want it."

The moment she said *Cambridge*, I was hooked. Maybe Dr. Armstrong knew Julian.

"How could I possibly fit a TA position into my schedule? It's already so full."

She waved her hand. "I doubt you'll have much work to do. He doesn't want a TA. It's in his contract, but I'm sure he'll make an exception for you."

"What makes you so sure he'll do that? Especially if he doesn't want someone to assist him."

She sat back and cleared her throat. "You're a beautiful girl, Meghan. I'm sure you won't have a hard time convincing Dr. Armstrong to allow you to assist him."

My eyes narrowed, because what she suggested was insane. "Are you serious? You want me to seduce him?"

"I didn't say that."

"No, but it was implied."

"Listen, Meghan. Do you want to graduate on time or not?"

"Of course, I do."

"Then accept what I'm offering you."

I was officially between a rock and a hard place. With no other option, I agreed, and Dr. Francis provided me with Dr. Armstrong's lecture schedule. At least I had a few hours to work on my plan of seduction before his first lecture.

And now, here I stand like a complete idiot, with my hot British summer fling staring me right in the face.

"Julian?" My voice is almost a gasp.

I want to run and wrap myself around him, but I resist because fifty freshman students are gaping at us.

"You're my teaching assistant? What in the bloody hell do they think they're doing?" His deep voice is like silk gliding over my body, sending goosebumps up my arms.

I look around the room, double checking that all eyes are still on us. "I guess so."

He clears his throat and shakes his head. "We will discuss this with Dr. Francis after my lecture."

He wets his index finger between his lips and peels off a syllabus from the stack on the table in front of him.

Jesus, the places his mouth has been.

He holds the packet out to me, and I walk slowly toward him. I'm so eager for any kind of contact, I almost trip on my way to take it.

"Have a seat in the back and read through this." He's professional now, snatching his hand away as soon as I have the syllabus.

He begins his lecture without missing a beat, and I hurry to find an empty seat in the back of the lecture hall. I settle into my seat as quietly as possible before giving him my full attention.

How could I not? The man is academic sex on a stick. His dark hair is neatly styled, and I spy the strands of silver close to his temples. My fingers flex as I remember how thick his hair felt gripped tightly in my hands.

The sleeves of his white button-down shirt are

already rolled up, revealing muscled forearms, and his navy-blue trousers fit his trim waist perfectly. Silently, I pray for him to turn around because the man has the ass of a god.

My eyes flick around the room, taking notice of the way every student is paying attention to Julian. They're hanging on every word coming from his delicious, devilish mouth. All he's doing is providing them with a bit of context about Shakespeare's background, but the smooth baritone of his voice is demanding enough to earn their attention.

My body trembles at the memory of him using a similar tone with me, gently commanding me to kneel before him. I was so eager and willing to please him, to do anything for one touch, one kiss. It didn't take him long to have me eating out of the palm of his hand.

And it doesn't take him long to have these students enamored.

I was sent on a mission to seduce Dr. Armstrong into accepting me as his new TA, but it seems too easy.

No, I won't be seducing Dr. Julian Armstrong. I'll be on my knees, begging him for a second chance.

CHAPTER THREE

JULIAN

I spend most of the lecture avoiding eye contact with Meghan. I cannot believe Stephanie sent her to be my teaching assistant. Not only did I explicitly say I did not need one, but Meghan told me she was a professor here, not a student. Shame on me for being fooled.

No matter how much I want her, it's impossible now. Being in a relationship with a student is the fastest way to tank my entire career.

"Read Shakespeare's Sonnet 18 and be prepared to discuss it during the next lecture." I immediately place my copy of the sonnets on the podium as the class files quickly out of the lecture hall.

I pinch the bridge of my nose to keep my

composure; there is no doubt Meghan will want to speak with me at the end of class. As if on cue, I feel her before I hear the melody of her voice calling my name.

"Julian?"

"It's Dr. Armstrong," I snap as I release my nose.

I have to grip the podium to stop myself from falling. She is even more beautiful than I remember. The scent of roses and honey wafts through the air as she steps closer.

"Jul...Dr. Armstrong, how have you been doing? It's been a while since we last talked."

"Do you really think we can just pick up where we left off?"

Meghan flinches as if I've hit her.

"What are you playing at, Meghan? You lied to me. Clearly, you're not a professor here, like you said. So, you're what, a student? And you want to be my TA?"

"I'm sorry. I know there isn't anything I can do to apologize for lying to you, but would you have even given me a chance if you knew I was twenty-one?"

She places her hand on top of mine, but I snatch it away.

"I'm sorry." Meghan bows her head, but not before I notice a single tear traveling down her cheek.

"I'm sorry, too. No matter how much I want this, nothing can happen between us. I came here for you, but I have a reputation to protect."

Her head snaps up. "You came all the way here for me?"

A glimmer of hope shows in her eyes, but no matter how much I want her, it's just not possible.

"Did. Past tense. Like I said, Meghan, there is no longer anything between us." I sigh. "I'll talk to Dr. Francis and figure out another class for you to TA. I neither want nor need a TA in this class. I could teach it with my eyes closed."

"Please don't. This is my only chance to graduate on time."

"That doesn't seem to be my problem. Maybe you should have worked harder at Cambridge instead of lying to me."

I don't wait for her response and head directly for the door. Stephanie and I need to talk.

My harsh words replay in my mind as I head toward Stephanie's office. No matter what happened between Meghan and me, I shouldn't have lashed out at her. No matter how much her lies hurt me, she deserves to be heard. Maybe after I calm down, we can have a rational conversation that doesn't end with the two of us in bed together.

I stop in front of Stephanie's office, knocking gently on the door. Hopefully, this meeting with her will be productive, and then I can be rid of Meghan and move on.

"Come in," she calls from the other side of the door.

She's sitting behind her desk, waiting as if she knew what my response would be to her assigning Meghan to be my TA.

"I thought I made myself explicitly clear during our negotiations. I was not to have a TA, but perhaps you forgot." My words are terse as I slowly sink into the chair across from Stephanie's desk.

"I sincerely apologize, Julian, but a situation arose with Meghan's credits, and this was the only option I could think of." She leans forward, causing her blouse to dip just enough to show her breasts.

She smiles pleasantly, her red lips revealing perfectly white teeth. I roll my eyes. Why do some women find it necessary to use sex to manipulate men? I'm thinking I should've stayed in Cambridge.

"There has to be some other way to help her. I absolutely refuse to have a TA. They're nothing but trouble, and I don't have the time to properly train one."

Stephanie places her palms flat on the desk and pushes herself up to stand. "Maybe we can come to a little arrangement."

She saunters around the desk and comes to a stop right in front of me before she bends forward and places her hands on each arm of the chair. She looks up at me with big brown eyes and a devious smirk on her lips, and her tongue darts out, slowly licking across her lips.

"I want you, Julian. I worked long and hard to get the Board of Directors to finally offer you this position. Now that I have you, I won't let you go. I'll do whatever it takes to make you happy."

She sinks to her knees in front of me and drags her hands down my knees. Stephanie is an attractive woman, but desperation rolls off her in waves.

"I'm sorry, but I make it a point to never get involved with my colleagues," I say.

"I'm sure you can make an exception just this once." She sits up and leans forward, running her hands up my thighs to the waistband of my trousers, then reaching out to grasp my belt buckle between her fingers.

Just as I'm ready to push her away, I hear a

knock on her door, and someone turns the knob to enter.

"Oh, Christ," I mutter when I see the first flash of brilliant blue.

CHAPTER FOUR

I must be the biggest fool on the planet. Lying to Julian was wrong, but my desire for him was so strong that I was willing to do anything to have him. Even pretend to be someone else. What harm was there if all we had was a summer fling? I never expected him to accept a position at Danville because of me.

But he wants nothing to do with me and refuses to let me be his TA, which puts my graduation status in jeopardy. On top of that, my capstone project is currently dead in the water. Stephanie rejected my proposed topic after I returned from Cambridge, and now I have to start from scratch.

Despite my somber mood, I head to Stephanie's office to give her the bad news. No doubt she'll be angry with me, but I can't force Julian to accept something—or some*one*—he doesn't want. If summer school is my only option, then I have no choice but to take it.

But when I knock on Stephanie's door and turn the handle, I'm shocked to see her in front of Julian, on her knees with her hands wrapped around his belt.

Fucking bitch.

"What the hell?" she screeches, scrambling to her feet. "What makes you think you can just barge in here?"

"I-I-I'm sorry," I stutter. "I wasn't thinking."

"Obviously," she snaps as she straightens her blouse and sits down behind her desk with a huff. "You'll have to come back later, Meghan."

The air in the room is heavy with tension, and I shift nervously on my feet. I'm feeling too many emotions and I'd rather get this ugly mess out of the way.

"Actually…" I say with a quick glance toward Julian. "I'm glad Dr. Armstrong is here. He doesn't want a TA, so we need to make another arrangement."

"Well, it doesn't matter what Dr. Armstrong

wants, because he is a guest at Danville University, and I've assigned him a TA."

"Absolutely not!" Julian bellows, jumping to his feet. "We have a contract! If you break our agreement, I'll have no choice but to file a grievance with the union."

The smile Stephanie plasters on her face is fake as fuck. I recognize it easily enough because it's the same one sorority sisters use to your face right before they stab you in the back.

"I apologize, Dr. Armstrong, but we put our students first here, and Meghan's graduation is in jeopardy."

"I don't give a damn whether she graduates. You offered me a position, which I accepted with certain parameters. Now, either honor my contract or I'll be on the next flight back to London."

Stephanie's cheeks flush, but I'm not sure whether it's from embarrassment or anger. "This is only a temporary problem, Dr. Armstrong. I'll talk to the board tonight to see if they'll agree to extra compensation. Now, if you'll both excuse me, I have a meeting to attend."

She looks at us expectantly until finally Julian relents and leaves. I follow him, hurrying to catch up.

"Julian, wait!" I hiss, hoping my voice is loud enough for him to hear.

I'm desperate to talk, to explain why I lied and why I stopped returning his emails.

He stops abruptly, spins on his heel, and walks into an empty classroom. Like a lovesick puppy, I scurry after him.

The moment I cross the threshold, the door slams shut, and Julian has me pinned against the wall. Closing my eyes, I inhale his familiar clean, spicy scent and the mint of his breath. My hands shoot out and grab his shirt.

"Julian," I breathe out.

His hands skim my waist before they wrap around mine and push them away. "What do you think you're doing, Meghan?"

"Give me a chance to explain," I beg.

"Why?"

"Because I'm in love with you," I confess.

He laughs. "In love with me? Love isn't built on lies, Meghan. Clearly, you're too young and stupid to understand that."

His words sting like a sharp slap across the face, but I refuse to submit to his cruelty.

"I understand you're angry with me, but you

don't have to be an asshole. Lying about my age is nothing compared to the lies you've told."

"You're accusing me of lying?" He steps away and paces the small classroom.

"Yes! You're not the same man I met in Cambridge. That man wouldn't treat me so callously."

He runs his hands through his hair, grabbing at the strands. "Because I thought you were someone else, Meghan! I thought we were colleagues."

"Why can't you see I'm the same person, Julian? The only thing I was dishonest about was my age. Everything else was real."

His face softens and his hands drop to his sides. For a moment, I think he's going to forgive me, and briefly, I fantasize about his arms wrapped around me tightly and his lips rebranding mine with his searing kiss.

An idea comes to mind. It's a risk, but it's worth taking. My mouth opens and I speak the one word I hope will turn things around.

"Daddy."

Julian's head pops up and his eyes widen. "What did you say?"

"Daddy," I repeat.

His nostrils flare and he turns away from me to

pace the room, his face constantly changing with emotion until, at last, he stops and bangs his fist down on the desk.

"Why are you doing this to me?"

"Because I still want you, and if there's even a chance you feel the same, then I'm going to take it."

I wait for the angry outburst. Instead, his words are soft.

"I'm sorry, but I'm nearly twenty years older than you, Meghan. Had I known the truth this summer, I would've stayed away, which is exactly what I'm going to do now."

Out of frustration, I stamp my foot. "You're acting as if I'm some underage teenager, Julian. I'm a grown woman."

"No, you're not. A twenty-one-year-old girl is just that: a *girl*. And I don't get involved with girls for any reason." Julian steps forward and slips one hand around my waist, leaning forward slightly and brushing his lips against mine. "I'm sorry, Meghan. Truly."

In the blink of an eye, he's gone, and my heart cracks open.

CHAPTER FIVE

JULIAN

Sometimes, being a morally conscious prick is hard. But it's the right thing to do, no matter how much I ache to be inside Meghan one more time. I never get involved with my colleagues, and I'd certainly never sleep with a student. Even a TA.

Still, something feels off about this whole situation.

It's regret. I don't have many, but when it comes to the way I spoke to Meghan and the way I cruelly cast aside her needs for the sake of my own, I wish I could do it all again.

Stephanie keeps calling, but I send them all right to voicemail. The way she acted was utterly unprofessional. She should be reported to the Board of Directors for sexual harassment, but what's the point? I'm not a permanent faculty member. I'm merely a guest here to enlighten the minds of Danville University's freshman class.

Even with all the distractions, I teach one more class before the end of my first official day. The Bard always has a way of soothing my soul.

So does having a beautiful woman whisper "yes, Daddy" as I drive my cock deep into her.

I shake my head. *Fuck.*

There are only two things that can purge me of these desires: whiskey and pounding the pavement.

Since Americans know fuck-all about the former, I choose the latter.

The quaint New England town of Danville exists only because of the university, so the campus and the city center are one and the same. With my trainers firmly tied, I set off for a run.

But it's no use. I can't shake Meghan from my thoughts. It's as if she's with me wherever I go. It's almost as if she's right in front of me.

I nearly trip as I come to a halt, because Meghan *is* in front of me, a few meters away, stumbling from the front door of a brick Victorian with some prick chasing her.

"Wait! Don't go!" he calls out, reaching for her.

His hand closes around her arm, and he pulls, spinning her. "I'm sorry, okay?"

"No, it's not okay!" she screeches as she swats his hand away. "Don't fucking touch me, you perv!"

"Oy!" I yell, sprinting toward them. "What's the problem?"

Meghan covers her face with her hands. "Oh, Jesus. Can't a girl catch a break?"

"Hey, mind your business, Dumbledore."

Dumbledore? What the fuck? This wanker certainly wants his arse beat, but one glance toward Meghan, and I see tears streaming down her cheeks. Sod it.

"She *is* my business."

I approach her slowly, but she grunts with frustration and stomps away.

"Just get the fuck away from me, Julian!"

"Hey!" I call out, chasing her. "I just want to talk."

She spins on her heel and faces me, her blue eyes ablaze. "Oh, now you want to talk, *Dr. Armstrong*? My life is a fucking mess right now, but you *finally* want to talk."

I turn back toward the Victorian-style house, where there's clearly a party happening, and spot a small crowd gathered out front.

"Just settle down. You're obviously pissed off."

"You're damn right I'm pissed!"

She trips over her feet, but I'm right there to catch her before she hits the pavement. She looks up at me with a scowl and shakes herself free of my grip.

"Isn't this how a twenty-one-year-old-*girl* is supposed to act, Julian?"

"Meghan, please…"

"Please what? Please don't act like a child?" She drops her bag to the ground, grips the hem of her T-shirt and lifts it, revealing her perfect *bare* breasts to everyone watching us. "Is *this* childish enough for you, Dr. Armstrong?"

"Fuck," I growl before rushing toward her and shielding her with my body.

There are hoots and hollers coming from behind us, awakening the green-eyed beast inside me.

Mine, he silently roars.

"What the bloody hell are you doing?"

"Just acting my age," she says innocently.

"Yeah, well, I've a mind to take you over my knee and smack your arse red."

"Promises, promises," she mocks.

"Come on, Megs. Let's go back to my place and have a proper chat about all this."

She scowls. "Don't call me that."

"Fine, but we're going back to my place. Now, you can either walk there or I can carry you. Make your choice."

She doesn't make a move. I roll my eyes as I step forward and grab her around the waist before slinging her over my shoulder.

"Obstinate girl," I mutter, and for good measure, I lay a smack across one of her arse cheeks.

After a few blocks, she finally relents and begs me to put her down.

"You realize someone was probably recording your little fit," I scold her.

"Probably? They were definitely recording."

"Meghan, not only am I faculty at Danville, but I'm also a guest."

"Relax. You've only been here a day. No one even knows you."

I take a moment to study her. It feels like forever since I've seen her, and earlier in the day I didn't allow myself to truly enjoy having her back within my sight. She looks younger, but also tired. Her cheeks are flushed, but there are also dark circles under her eyes.

I frown. "Why do you look so tired?"

"Stress," she mutters as we walk toward the

converted Victorian where I'm renting a flat for the term.

Instinctively, I run my hand along her back and up her neck, letting my fingers tangle in her hair. Protectiveness and possessiveness surge to life inside me because deep down, I know Meghan is mine. Mine to protect. Mine to worship. Mine to punish.

But is she mine to love? I hadn't decided on that yet.

To my surprise, she doesn't run from my touch. Our steps fall in line, and she moves closer to me. We have a lot to discuss, but I can't deny how good it feels to have my hands on her again. Maybe I can cross the line for one night…if only to teach her a lesson.

CHAPTER SIX

MEGHAN

A jolt of electricity shoots down my spine as Julian's fingers gently stroke my skin. Memories of those fingers caressing other parts of my body make my skin heat and my thighs clench.

"Penny for your thoughts, little one?" His husky voice breaks the spell.

"Little one? I wasn't so little to you when you were fucking me against every available surface," I huff and pull from his grasp.

I turn to head back toward the party but am suddenly lifted over his shoulder again.

"That's what you are to me, Megs. *My* little one. And it seems you've forgotten," he growls as he places two more quick slaps across my ass.

The unexpected pleasure makes me gasp.

"Seems my little one might enjoy her punishment after all."

"Punishment for what? I've done nothing wrong. Now, put me down and stop treating me like a damn child."

I squirm to relieve some of the ache in my core. I will not admit I enjoyed his little display of dominance. It's one thing to have a little fun in the bedroom, but it's a whole different situation to treat me like a child in public.

"Squirm all you want, Meghan. I'm not putting you down until we are inside my flat. It's time for you to learn your lesson, one I should have taught you when I first discovered your lies."

Julian strides toward his place as if I weigh nothing. He carries me inside and up the stairs, taking them two at a time until he reaches the front door of his apartment. The door opens effortlessly as we enter.

"I know you're not used to having to lock your door at night, but this isn't the safest area," I get out before Julian throws me down on the couch.

"My only intention when I left was a quick run. I didn't know there was a naughty little girl waiting for me to come punish her."

There is a fire in his eyes I've never seen before. I'm tempted to push harder, to see if I can get him to break his calm exterior and show me the passion I saw over the summer. But even if he does, the truth will remain: I'm still not good enough.

"You sound like my father." I roll my eyes. "Although I'm grateful you were there to chase off Captain Douche, I would have eventually handled it myself."

"I'm well aware you can take care of yourself, but now that I'm here, you don't have to." He presses a gentle kiss on my forehead and turns to head toward the kitchen.

I gave this man my heart once before and he broke it into a million pieces. If I let him in again, I'm not sure I'll survive.

Julian returns and hands me a cold bottle of water.

"Sit up," he commands gently before sitting beside me.

He holds out his hand, which contains two white pills, and I glance up at him briefly.

"Aspirin," is all he says.

I swallow down the medicine, but remain quiet. If I tell Julian about my impromptu date, Max, he'll go nuts. It's hard for me to admit, but I'm grateful to Julian for swooping in and saving the day.

"Tell me what happened," he softly urges me.

"There's really nothing to say," I lie.

Julian squeezes my thigh, a clear sign demanding honesty.

I sigh. "Fine. I met up with that guy at the party. We've had classes together over the years, and when he called to invite me, I went. I didn't realize Max was such a handsy asshole."

Julian's hand tightens on my leg, and I hear him growl under his breath.

"To be fair, we both had way too much to drink. I was trying to forget all about you."

"Don't," Julian barks. "Don't excuse what he did to you."

"He didn't do anything. One sloppy kiss and I was out of there."

Julian pops up from the couch.

"He *kissed* you?" His roar fills the small room, and I shrink back against the couch. He looks down at me and his anger softens slightly. "Did you give him permission?"

"No," I admit.

"Bloody hell, Megs. That's fucking sexual assault."

Hot tears sting my eyes. "It was stupid, I know. I've never willingly put myself in a situation like that before. But I wanted to forget everything that had happened earlier. I thought I lost you for good."

Julian sits back down beside me, and I turn to face him. His handsomeness takes my breath away. How did I end up with someone like him? I'm just a nobody from Scottsdale, Arizona who somehow caught the eye of a handsome British professor.

He leans forward and brushes my hair back behind my shoulder.

"You haven't lost me, little one," he says with a purr before brushing his lips against mine. "I just needed to figure out a new way for us to exist together."

"And have you?"

One corner of his mouth tips up. "Not quite, but nothing clears my head like a good punishment."

He scoots away and sits up straight before patting his knee.

"You can't be serious?" I ask incredulously.

Over the summer, we only engaged in a little light spanking. He never seriously punished me. Maybe because we were only a temporary thing. Or maybe because I was on my best behavior.

"I'm very serious, little one. You've been very

naughty, and my palm is itching to turn your arse red."

CHAPTER SEVEN

I wait patiently for her to bend herself over my knee, but there is nothing but indecision in her eyes.

"Either you willingly go over my knee or I put you over it, but I will punish you tonight, little one."

"Punish me?' What for?" Meghan crosses her arms over her chest, and my cock hardens.

I've always loved her bratty attitude and her need to challenge me at every turn, but this is serious. That little prick could've easily done a lot more than just try and steal a kiss.

"Because you need to understand what you did wrong."

"Oh, so because you're jealous someone else

was able to spend time with me, you want to spank me." Meghan storms toward me, smashing her finger into my chest. "You are out of your mind if you think I'm going to let you spank me like a child. Sure, I let things get out of hand with Max and you had to come to my rescue, but I don't deserve to be punished."

"The hard way it is." With her tiny wrists grasped in my hand, I pull her over my knee despite her defiant squirming. "Sit still, or your punishment will last longer."

I smooth my hands over her round, luscious bottom before giving it two quick but sharp blows. "You're being punished because I could've lost you."

My through clogs with emotion as images of the horrible thing he could've done to her, all because she trusted the wrong man, fill my mind. I know I can't forbid her from seeing other people, although I'd love to keep her locked in this flat under my protection, away from the world and all the horrible people that inhabit it. But that's not going to fly with my little one.

"Unbutton your shorts for me. There's no way you aren't getting bare skin this time around."

"You're serious?" she questions, turning her head to look up at me.

"Little one." I clench my eyes shut, trying to find the words to explain. "I need this as much as you do. I need you to understand how dangerous what you did was, but I also need this for me. To remind myself that you're here, safe, and with me."

He entire demeanor softens as she shimmies her shorts down her arse. "I'm sorry, Daddy."

I bite my lip to stifle the moan wanting to escape my lips. My cock grows hard at just the thought of turning her bottom red.

"Someone is excited," Meghan purrs as she rubs her hand over the growing bulge, attempting to distract me.

"Be careful, little one. Teasing me will only mean more punishment for you." I punctuate my statement with the crack of my hand against her bottom.

"Fuck, that hurt," she groans, bucking off my lap.

"That's the point of the punishment, little one. It's supposed to hurt. Sometimes we need to be reminded who is in charge." My right hand is firm against her back, holding her in place while my left comes down quickly across her newly pink skin.

Smack. Smack. Smack.

"Do you plan on being more careful in the future?" My hand runs over her cherry-red cheeks before my fingers dip into her folds. "Someone seems to be enjoying her . punishment, just as I thought you would, little one."

I quickly plunge one finger in and out, and each time, her pussy grips my finger.

"Oh, Julian, that feels so good. More, please."

"I love it when you beg, baby, but I asked you a question." I deny her pleasure until she answers and place a stinging smack to remind her tonight is all about punishment. "Are you going to scare Daddy like that again? I wouldn't survive is something happened to you."

"Yes, I promise I'll be good."

"Damn right you will. Who do you belong to?" I slide my fingers in between her folds, pumping in and out swiftly, bringing moans of pleasure from her lips.

"I belong to you. You and only you. Please don't stop."

She pushes her arse up toward my hand to get more friction, but I pull back. I would love nothing more than to drive my cock deep inside her, sending us both into oblivion, but she needs to learn her place.

"Don't stop, Julian! I'm so close. Please don't stop." The walls of her pussy clench around my fingers, signaling her need for release.

I pull my fingers out and bring them to my lips, licking her juices from them. She needs to understand her behavior is unacceptable. No other man but me is to touch her.

"Please! Don't stop, Julian! I'll do whatever you want. Just let me come!" Meghan begs, sitting up and wrapping herself around me, grinding her soaking wet pussy on my hard cock.

It's hard for me to deny her because, in turn, I'm denying myself the pleasure of her wet core sliding down my shaft.

"Shhh, little one. It's over now; you made me so proud." I smile, like a proud father. "This is a lesson you needed to learn."

"Are you fucking kidding me? What do you mean, it's over? I let you spank me so hard I probably won't be able to sit down for a week." Meghan reaches for her shorts and knickers from the floor.

I'm quicker, though, and snatch them before she has the chance to grab them. "I'll be keeping these."

"Whatever gets you off, asshole," she says curtly.

"Little one, I don't need to spank you to know I own you." I push off the couch, standing to my full height as she pulls up her shorts and buttons them. Leaning forward, I whisper in her ear. "Don't pretend that every smack on your arse didn't turn you on. I felt your pussy clench around my fingers. You're a greedy little girl. You loved receiving your punishment as much as I loved administering it. If you had asked me to stop, I would have stopped. Don't let your anger make you say something you'll regret in the morning."

The look of defiance in her eyes makes me want to pull her over my knee again, but I don't. She is angry and maybe a little confused, but she needs to sort her feelings out and quickly.

"Megs, this is who I am, and I've never pretended to be anything else. When you misbehave, you will be punished."

While looking me straight in the eye, Meghan motions me closer. I smirk as I step forward, knowing how stubborn she is.

When I'm close enough, she raises up on tiptoes and whispers, "Yes, Daddy."

Then she brushes a kiss on my cheek before sashaying out of my house.

It isn't until the front door closes that the shock of what she just said wears off, and I let out a boisterous laugh.

"Well played, little one. Well played."

She may not have knowledge of what it means to be my little girl, but she already has me wrapped around her finger.

CHAPTER EIGHT

MEGHAN

I do not have daddy issues. But when Julian dominates me, something inside me comes to life, and that's what I needed tonight. Except now I'm home alone without my panties, with a sore, chafed ass. The toy inside the drawer of my nightstand is tempting, but it's no match for the real thing. I can wait; Julian will eventually give me what I want because he wants it too.

There is still the little problem of being his assistant, though. There has got to be a reason for his stubbornness.

I wake up earlier than usual this morning and head to the only cafe in town for Julian's favorites: sweet milky tea and flaky croissants. The only time over the summer I saw him eat anything remotely close to junk food was at breakfast.

After stopping at the cafe, I head to his apartment, careful not to spill the scalding hot tea all over my pristine white blouse. I stick the wax pastry bag between my teeth and knock on Julian's door.

He doesn't answer. I roll my eyes and knock harder, because he's not a late sleeper.

I hear heavy footsteps on the old hardwood floors and the front door to the converted Victorian opens. Slowly, I turn and come face-to-face with a sweaty, shirtless Julian.

Holy fuck.

"Is that for me?" He nods toward the tray in one hand.

Like an idiot, I mumble the answer, with the bag firmly clenched between my teeth. He chuckles softly and grabs the bag, and we head toward his apartment door.

"To what do I owe the pleasure?" he asks as he unlocks the door before opening it wide.

I make it a point to inhale his fresh, manly scent as I pass.

You're here for information, I remind myself as I place the cardboard carrier on the small dining table.

But as soon as I glance back at Julian, still sweaty and shirtless, my mission is forgotten entirely.

He opens the bag and the slight smile on his face widens into a full-blown grin. He plucks out the croissant and takes a hearty bite, then looks back inside, and his smile disappears.

"There's only one. Didn't you get one for yourself?"

No, 'cause my head is entirely filled with you, I answer silently.

Slowly, he stalks his way toward me, discarding the bag to the floor. When he's right in front of me, he tears off a piece of the pastry and holds it against my lips.

"I don't want you to starve, little one," he purrs.

I take a bite and chew slowly, my eyes locked completely on him. There's desire and temptation in his gaze, and fantasy combined with flashback flicker in my thoughts.

"Are you having the same thoughts?" He presses one hand against my chest and pushes me gently until my back hits the wooden table. His hand drags down my front to the waistband of my skirt, which makes him hum. "You're making this too easy on me."

"Or my ass hurts too bad for a pair of pants," I reply.

He slips a hand under my skirt and around my behind. "Tell me how I can make you feel better."

I groan because he *knows* what I want. He's just toying with me. He pulls his hand away and flips up my skirt, revealing the only pair of cotton panties I own. He sucks in a sharp breath before bending down to bury his nose between my thighs. The tickle of his hot breath makes me whimper and squirm.

"I'm losing patience," he murmurs before kissing the inside of one thigh. "Are you still mine, little one? Completely?"

"Yes," I whisper, arching my back slightly and pressing myself against him.

His hands travel up my body, gripping my waist. "Will you be a good girl and do exactly as I say?"

"Yes." My voice is a needy moan.

"All you have to do is say the word, little one, and you'll get exactly what you came here for."

My eyes pop open. Am I really getting what I want? There's only one way to find out.

"Daddy."

It's like a switch flip inside Julian. He releases

me and steps away, his back tall and straight, his eyes dark and dangerous.

"On your knees, little one," he commands.

I straighten and scramble to the floor. He moves directly in front of me while his hands slide beneath the waistband of his running shorts, and he shoves them down his thighs. His impressive cock juts out, already hard and ready. My mouth waters, but I wait for his order.

He runs a gentle hand over my head and down my cheek until it cups my jaw. His thumb brushes my bottom lip until, at last, he speaks.

"Open your mouth."

Instantly, I obey. He grips the shaft of his cock loosely in his fist and runs the head over my lips before slipping inside. The command to close comes a second later, and I hear him sigh.

"Your mouth feels like heaven, little one."

I don't dare lick or suck until he tells me what he wants. This is how he does things. Daddy gets what he wants, and if he's satisfied, he rewards his little one. I'm eager to please.

"Make Daddy come."

My body relaxes as I reach a hand up to take hold of his cock. I swirl my tongue around the head before I swallow every inch of him. When the tip hits the back of my throat, I breathe through the gag reflex and hold him there for a second before releasing him and my breath.

He groans appreciatively. I repeat the action until his cock hardens against my tongue.

"Fuck," he hisses before he clamps his hands on either side of my head, holding it steady while his cock pistons in and out of my mouth.

He releases me and a little of his control. My cheeks hollow as I suck the head sharply before letting it pop out. Precum leaks from the tip and I lap it up, eager for every drop.

One hand wraps loosely around his shaft, guiding it back into my mouth while the other hand cups his balls. I look up just as he throws his head back and lets out a feral moan.

I know what you like, I tell him silently.

My mouth worships his cock, sucking and licking it until he tenses. He groans through the first wave of his orgasm as the first hot streams of his release hit the back of my tongue. His cock pulses as I drain the last drops from him.

After a minute, Julian sighs and slips from my mouth. His cock is still semi-hard, and when I glance up, there's a look of pure satisfaction on his face.

"I've missed your mouth, little one," he whispers as he runs his hands through my hair. "But you know what I've missed even more. Your sweet little pussy."

I sigh with relief because my core is aching for him to fill me. I want to press my thighs together to relieve some of the tension, but his reward will be so much greater if I wait. And I've been patient long enough.

CHAPTER NINE

I'm a man with a one-track mind. Meghan's waiting pussy calls out to me like a siren, but my mouth waters remembering her sweet, sinful taste.

"Up onto the table, little one. Daddy's still hungry."

Her lips form a devilish smile as she follows my command. Such an obedient little thing.

"Are you going to take care of this aching pussy, Daddy?" She pouts, playfully puckering her lips and batting her eyes seductively.

My cock hardens at the sight of her, so ready and eager for me. I shove my gym shorts down my thighs and toe off my trainers as I step closer to the table.

"Doesn't Daddy always take care of you, little one?"

"Yes," Meghan hisses as her eyes close and her hand sneaks its way toward her core.

Swatting her hand, I admonish her. "No touching. Spread your legs and let Daddy have his breakfast."

A loud moan fills the room as she spreads her legs wide and I kneel before her, ready to worship at her feet. I breathe in her aroma as I bury my nose in her damp knickers.

"*Mm*, you're going to be the best meal I've had in months. I'll never get enough of you, little one."

Pulling her knickers to the side, I slowly drag my tongue between her folds, taking her swollen clit between my lips and sucking it deep into my mouth. My eyes roll into the back of my head as I groan when her flavor hits my tastebuds. That possessiveness I feel for her comes raging to the surface, consuming me. The need to claim her as my own overwhelms but I need to take my time. I want to savor this moment and brand it into my memory for years to come. After all the trials that we've been through to get here, it's been worth every minute. I wouldn't change a thing, other than the time we spent apart. Meghan is my everything, my little one, and I'm never letting her go again.

She squirms against me, lifting her hips.

"That's not how we get what we want, is it?"

She replies with only a whimper as I shove two fingers into her drenched center, scissoring them open and closed. She gasps with pleasure as I watch her chase the first of many orgasms. I lean forward and suck her clit between my lips, rolling my tongue over the stiff bundle of nerves and pulling it further and further into my mouth until her entire body shakes and she bucks away.

Although I would love to feast on her for eternity, patience was never a virtue I mastered. I need to feel her pussy clench around my aching cock.

"Are you ready for Daddy, little one?"

"Yes, Daddy. Fuck me, please. Own me."

She always knows exactly what I want to hear. I step away briefly to grab a condom from my wallet and quickly sheath my cock before plunging it deep into her waiting pussy. Her back arches off the table as we both moan in pleasure. This is no time for gentleness. I need this. *We* need this. To know we are together. I will not lose her again.

My hand snakes its way up her body and stops at the base of her throat. My fingers flex before they wrap around it loosely, maintaining enough gentle pressure for her to know who is in control. Her walls constrict around me, clenching my cock tighter.

"You are the air I breathe, little one," I grit out.

Meghan is mine, and why I ever doubted it, I'll never know. Maybe I feared the emotions I was finally feeling for someone. Maybe I feared her rejection once she understood the full depths of my desires. But Meghan is my willing partner, eager to lose herself in our roleplay.

The table moves across the floor, scratching the beautiful hardwood, as I pound into her while her nails claw their way down my back.

"That's it, little one. Let go. I'll always keep you safe."

She cries out as her entire body tenses. I continue to punish her with my body, all the while whispering words of love into her ear, until at last, she screams from absolute pleasure.

"Come for me, little one. Come for Daddy," I whisper as she crashes into her orgasm.

"Oh, Julian! Daddy!" Her entire body quakes and quivers beneath me as tears stream down her cheeks.

Nothing can keep me away from her ever again.

It's not long after that I follow, hammering her pussy into submission one final time before climaxing so hard I see stars and nearly collapse on top of her. We both lie there in silence, sharing in a moment of pure contentment, and I feel her small fingers caressing my back.

"Did you mean it?" Her voice falters as if she fears the answer I'll give.

Propping myself up on my elbow, I look into her eyes and brush the sweat-matted tendrils of hair from her forehead. "There's only one reason I came to this bloody place. *You*. And I'll follow you to the ends of the earth if I must, but one thing is for certain. I'm never letting you go."

She sighs, and I'm given her beautiful smile, the one I know is only meant for me. I vow I will move Heaven and Earth for her, even if it means tarnishing my unblemished reputation.

"I'd love to sit here and fuck all day, but you need to get your education and I have a lecture to prepare. Seems I have a TA being forced on me. I'm going to need to whip her into shape." I push myself up off the table and head toward the bedroom.

"Julian, do you mean it? You'll let me be your TA?" Meghan jumps up from the table, her gorgeous tits bouncing.

The sight has me thinking of calling in sick on the second day of classes.

"It's Dr. Armstrong in class. Understand, little one?" I scold her with a pointed look.

Meghan crosses her arms directly under her breasts, pushing them once again into perfect view. "It's Meghan, Dr. Armstrong. Not 'little one.'"

I shake my head in defeat. This one is going to be a handful. I'm not sure how Meghan being my TA and us trying to make a go of being together is going to work out, but the idea of being the reason she doesn't graduate doesn't sit well with me.

"Touché. Now get your fine arse in the shower before I have my way with you again. I might be twenty years your senior, but I still fuck like a lad."

Meghan shakes her head, but as she passes by, I give her a swat on the arse for good measure.

"Don't sass me, little one."

"Yes, Daddy," she says over her shoulder before she scurries toward the bedroom.

I take my time following behind her. If I know Meghan, she won't wait for us to get in the shower. I'll have her at least once or twice in the bed before we even make it there. I glance down at the watch on my wrist. Plenty of time until my first lecture.

When I enter the bedroom, I spread Meghan out on the bed like a tantalizing treat.

"Dear me," I say. "Hope you don't have an early morning class, little one, because Daddy is ready for seconds."

CHAPTER TEN

MEGHAN

For the next few days, I don't leave Julian's apartment—or his bed—except to attend class. And I'm pretty sure when I show up, the smell of sex oozes from my pores.

But we're careful because Julian's reputation as a scholar is as important as my ability to graduate according to plan. That doesn't mean I don't enjoy tempting him with low-cut tops and skirts that skim my ass, though.

"You'd better watch yourself, little one," he growls into my ear after his last lecture for the day.

He reaches out and hooks my arm, dragging me toward him, then presses one hand to my back and pushes me down onto the table, where he keeps stacks of student essays. My chest is flat against the surface and I hear him hum behind me. His hand roams down my back and under my skirt.

"You've been wearing skirts like this a lot lately."

"Just for you, Daddy," I purr.

His hand wraps around the side of my panties and he yanks, tugging at the flimsy fabric until it tears away.

"Think you can keep quiet, little one?" he asks, showing me the black fabric balled up in his fist. "Or do you need help?"

"I'll be quiet, I promise."

He chuckles. "We'll see about that."

And then Julian tests my ability to remain quiet. There's no warning, not even the slightest hint, before he buries his cock deep in my pussy. It's heavenly and I moan loudly, earning my ass a sound smack.

"One more outburst and I'll stuff these between your gorgeous lips," he warns me.

I nod and do my best, but it's hard when Julian slams ruthlessly into me over and over.

I grip the edge of the table, pressing my ass against him. He grips my hips tightly, completely controlling the rhythm.

The papers beneath me shift until they fall to the floor. The sounds of our bodies slapping together and the light fluttering of paper fill the cavernous lecture hall. And then Julian adds more fuel to the fire.

"Touch yourself, little one," he demands. "Finger your clit while I fuck your pussy."

I look back at him because there's no way I'll be able to remain quiet.

"Open wide," he says before pressing the fabric against my lips.

Once he's satisfied the makeshift gag is in place, he repeats his previous command, emphasizing it with another loud crack on my ass.

One hand remains on the desk while the other slides between my slippery folds. I can feel his length against my fingers as his thick cock strains the walls of my pussy. Despite the fabric muffling any sound, I groan.

Holy fuck, this is dirty. And hot.

My fingers furiously work my clit, strumming it, teasing it, while Julian plunges in and out of me. He whispers filthy things into my ear, saying anything to ignite the powder keg inside me that's ready to blow.

"Come on, little one," he encourages me. "Come all over Daddy's cock."

My entire body tenses until I can't take any more. Until I thrust my ass against him, my eyes rolling back in my head. A loud whimpering moan escapes my lips and I'm sure I'll be punished. Anyone walking by could have heard that, but I don't care. All that matters is the powerful orgasm setting my body on fire.

I'm completely oblivious until Julian's frantic pounding jolts me back to reality. His hold on my hips is almost painful, but the discomfort doesn't last long. Julian roars through his own climax as his cock pulses, filling me with his seed.

"Fuck," he growls right before he slips out.

Despite my exhaustion, I feel empty. I crave a connection with Julian and when we're not together, I almost feel adrift. When I told him I loved him, he dismissed me, but I was being completely honest. And now that he's reclaimed me, my desire and affection for him have only grown.

Which makes me wonder about his feelings.

The word "love" has yet to escape his lips.

My obedience compels me to remain still until Julian has finished with me. He removes the makeshift gag from between my lips and uses the fabric to clean me, wiping away the signs of our tryst leaking from my center.

"Hmm," I hear him murmur before he sighs. "Can't bloody throw these in the bin, now, can I?"

I turn my head slightly to catch him pocketing my dirty panties.

"Come along, little one. You've got essays to sort, and I've got a lecture to prepare."

At last, I stand, wiggling the life back into my limbs. Julian comes around to stand opposite me, and from the look of him, you'd never know he just fucked me like an animal. Not a single hair is out of place and there is no sweat beading along his brow. The only sign is his slightly untucked shirt.

"You really have to stop teasing me, little one," he says with the quirk of his brow. "Can't have too many more of these slip-ups."

Over the next few days, there isn't time to be reckless. Stephanie hounds me about my revised capstone project, which I haven't even considered since the first day of school.

"I can't stay at your place tonight," I tell Julian after his last lecture.

His nostrils flare.

"We've discussed this, little one," he says sternly.

But tonight, I can't be his "little one." I need to be Meghan, the college senior.

"I really have to go back into my research and revise my capstone project. Stephanie has been bugging me for days. I can't keep brushing her off."

My dominant daddy softens. "Tell me how I can help, Megs."

I sigh. I love the way my names sound coming from his lips. "Thanks, but I need to do this myself. I don't want to be accused of academic dishonesty."

Before I can brush past him, he stops me with a firm hand on my shoulder. "Our relationship is about more than sex, little one. I'm here to make you happy, even if that means taking a night off from stuffing you full of my cock."

Laughter bubbles up and escapes my lips. "I really appreciate the offer, Julian. But I want to do this on my own."

Julian releases me, but doesn't let me pass. He leans against a nearby desk and crosses his arms over his broad chest.

"Fine. Then at least tell me your original topic and the reason Stephanie rejected it. If I think she's wrong, then I'll help you fight. If she's right, let me give you a few suggestions."

I sigh and give in to him. "Okay. I wanted to focus on the character of Ophelia and track all the various ways she's been portrayed."

"To what end?"

"To show she wasn't weak and mad, but trapped by the misogynistic society in which she lived. Her death was the only thing she could control."

He presses his index finger against his lips and is quiet for a moment. "And what did Stephanie say?"

"It's derivative. She said they've covered Ophelia ad nauseam."

"She's right." His words are unexpected. "Poor, poor mad Ophelia. Everyone wants to research her and dissect her. What else have you got?"

I shrug. "Nothing. I've always been drawn to Ophelia."

"You spent all that time at Cambridge researching one female character? Tsk, tsk, tsk."

"Not exactly. I also spent time on Desdemona."

His eyes light up.

"Now you're talking." Julian stands up straighter, steps forward, and grabs my hand. "Come on, little one. I'll draw you a nice, hot bath and we can spend the night discussing tragic romance. By morning, you'll have your capstone project sussed out."

His tone of voice makes me suspicious. He's far too chipper about all of this, and sex hasn't even been mentioned. He has something wicked planned. I just know it.

CHAPTER ELEVEN

L ast night with Meghan was amazing. As promised, I kept my hands to myself. I prepared dinner for us both before running a bath where we soaked away the day. But I'm no saint, and I couldn't let an opportunity with a wet, naked Meghan pass me by.

After much needed stress relief, we dove right into discussing Desdemona for Meghan's capstone thesis. Around two in the morning, we stumbled down the hall to the bedroom and passed out.

The birds chirping outside the window are an annoying reminder we're going to be late for class.

"We need to get moving, love, or we'll be late."

I stop short, catching my slip. I have loved Meghan from the moment she spilled hot tea in my lap, but we haven't uttered those few words to each other yet.

"I want to sleep a little longer, Daddy." Her whiny little voice comes from under my duvet.

I chuckle, throwing the duvet off us both and swinging my legs over the side of the bed before I stand. "Get up while I make tea. I didn't set the alarm this morning to give us a few extra hours, so unfortunately, no playtime."

There's a knock on the front door, and I wonder who in bloody hell is here this early in the morning.

"You'd better be out of this bed by the time I get back up here, or I'll be taking you over my knee."

"Promises, promises." Her voice follows me as I pull on a pair of sweatpants from the floor and head down the hall.

The mess we left in the living room—books, notes, and empty teacups—is all spread over the table in the center of the room. Ignoring it for a moment, I unlock and open the door to find Stephanie waiting with cherry-red lips and a Cheshire Cat smile.

"Good morning, Dr. Armstrong," she greets me as she shoves her way into the flat, shoving her bag and coat into my arms.

"To what do I owe the pleasure so early in the

morning?" My voice is tight as I try to hide my surprise and anger.

I glance quickly down the hall, hoping Meghan has enough sense to get dressed before coming out.

"You've been avoiding me." She looks around in disgust, taking in the scattered remnants of our late-night study session. "Too much work makes for a grumpy man."

Stephanie turns, giving me what I am sure is a playful smile. Instead, my anger increases.

"I'm a busy man."

I drop her belongings on the empty chair without another thought and continue my journey toward the kitchen. I need something stronger than tea to deal with her bullshit so early in the morning.

"I take mine black."

"I don't remember offering you a cuppa, but sure. Why not?" My manners seem to have temporarily left me. "Why are you here, Stephanie?"

I pour both of us a cup of coffee and turn, waiting for a response.

"I like a man who gets right to the point. All right, you've been putting off our dinner plans. I came to collect this morning. Since I make your schedule, I know you don't have class until this afternoon, and that you have a TA who would gladly take over office hours for you this morning."

Bollocks. I forgot all about the dinner invitation I agreed to earlier in the week. Stephanie is technically my boss, and I thought it only proper to indulge her.

Stephanie wraps her arms around my neck as she slides close to me. "It's time for you and I to get to know each other better, Dr. Armstrong."

At that moment, a loud bang signals Meghan's entry into the kitchen, and not wanting to make the same mistake twice, she ensures Stephanie is aware of her presence. "I'm so sorry, Dr. Armstrong! I didn't mean to fall asleep here last night. Thank you so much for helping me work out the issue with my capstone project. I'm sure Stephanie will be delighted to hear all the new developments at our appointment this morning."

Meghan has her claws out, ready to fight tooth and nail for her Daddy. There is no doubt in my mind that she heard most, if not all, of Stephanie's plans for her and me this morning. By the look in her eyes, she doesn't like it one bit.

"If you were more responsible with your time, you would have received my message cancelling our appointment this morning. I have plans with Dr.

Armstrong to discuss his future employment at Danville University." Stephanie unwraps her arms from around my neck and takes a step back.

I turn back toward the counter, unable to disguise the smirk on my face. "We can reschedule. Meghan worked very hard last night to prepare for your meeting this morning. I wouldn't want to stand in the way of her graduating on time, especially since that's the entire reason you forced me into having her as my teaching assistant."

With a huff, Stephanie stomps out of the kitchen in search of her bag, giving me the perfect opportunity to seize Meghan around the waist and purr into her ear. "Little one seems to be jealous. You know Daddy only has eyes for you."

Meghan twirls out of my grasp. "You've lost your mind, Julian! We almost got caught this morning. We need to be more careful. Are you sure she didn't come here for any other reason? Did she hint that she knew I was here?"

Meghan's chest rises and falls quickly. "Megs, take a deep breath. The only thing on that woman's mind when she arrived was my cock."

A small growl escapes her mouth, and I chuckle in response.

"Run along, little one, before she suspects something."

"Julian, we need to be more careful. If you lose your position because of me, I'll never forgive myself."

Before I have the chance to kiss some sense back into Meghan, Stephanie comes barreling back into the kitchen.

"Come along. I squeezed some time in for you between now and another meeting with the head of the romance languages department at eleven. If we hurry, we can finish, and all of us can make it to campus in time for Dr. Armstrong's office hours."

Meghan's face instantly transforms from sorrow to fake gratitude. "Thank you so much! Julian, can you please help me ensure all my notes are in order to present to Stephanie?"

"How dare you address Dr. Armstrong in such an informal manner? Show him the respect he deserves as an esteemed visiting faculty member from Cambridge!"

Meghan's face instantly pinkens in embarrassment. "My apologies, Dr. Armstrong. It won't happen again."

Before I can utter a word in her defense, she scurries out of the room.

"Someone needs to teach that girl some manners. I understand I let her call me by my first name, but I've known her for the past four years. Being an advisor to a student adds a level of familiarity."

"I encourage my students to use my first name when addressing me. I feel it fosters better communication."

Stephanie looks at me with a condescending smile. "That's just adorable. No wonder she has such a crush on you. I suggest you nip that in the bud, and soon, or you may have another problem on your hands."

This entire time, my blood has been simmering, but now it boils with rage as I process Stephanie's actions and words. First, she barges into my home, then she makes another sexual pass at me before insulting Meghan and insinuating I'd sleep with a student.

"How dare *you* speak to one of my students in that manner, especially in my home? If I ever hear you disrespect someone so rudely again, I'll report you and your behavior to the Dean of Students. Furthermore, I have entertained your sexual advances as a colleague, but you've shown that not only do you have no self-respect, but you have no respect for others as well. Next time you so much as look in my direction inappropriately, I will file a sexual harassment suit against you and the entire university."

Stephanie stares at me, speechless, for a few moments before nodding in the affirmative.

"If you will excuse me, I'm going to ensure Meghan has everything she needs for her presentation." Without another word, I turn on my heel and head toward the living room where I'll find my little one, the only person in this world who can calm the storm raging inside me.

CHAPTER TWELVE

MEGHAN

"Well, you and Dr. Armstrong have developed quite the working relationship," Stephanie says as she sits down in the chair behind her desk.

"I realized he might be able to help me with my project," I tell her as honestly as possible.

Julian was a tremendous help last night, asking me hard questions, forcing me to revise and refine my thesis until at last, my project came to life. When we went to bed, I was exhausted but confident, eager for my meeting.

Until Stephanie showed up unexpectedly at Julian's apartment and then, shit got really awkward.

"Yes, perhaps you want him to help you in more than one way," she sneers with one raised eyebrow.

I don't take the bait. "I don't know what you're talking about, but I'm eager to discuss my project with you."

She sits back in her chair, purses her lips, and narrows her eyes. "You're either incredibly naïve or incredibly smart. I haven't decided which."

When I don't engage her, she continues.

"You've got to be fucking Julian Armstrong. Did you ask him to write your thesis? Do all the work for you?"

I stand up, angry at her baseless accusations. "I've worked hard on this project! I researched my ass off this summer and spent *hours* in the libraries while I was at Cambridge."

She smiles widely, as though she discovered a hidden treasure. "You studied at Cambridge this summer!"

"Yes, of course. You approved my study abroad request."

"And you never ran into Dr. Armstrong during your trip?"

"N-no, I didn't." I trip over my words and glance away, hoping she doesn't catch sight of my red cheeks.

Stephanie hums. "Leave your revised proposal on my desk. I'll look over it and get back to you."

I face her, my eyes wide. "You aren't willing to talk it over and approve it now?"

"No, I'm not. Besides, I'd hate to further embarrass you when I run your thesis through the university's plagiarism checker."

Reluctantly, I reach into my backpack and pull out the folder with my work. I place it on her desk before leaving her office.

With my eyes on the ugly linoleum floor, I almost run right into Julian.

"What are you doing here?" I whisper as he pulls me down an empty hallway.

"How did it go?"

My shoulders slump as I sag against him. "I have no idea how she knows about us, but she does."

Julian's arms wrap tightly around me, holding me close, keeping me safe, comforting me. It's exactly what I needed after my disastrous meeting.

"She's far too blinded by her desire for me. She's grasping at straws, hoping to come up with a winner."

I look up into his gaze. "My entire future is in her hands."

His large hands brush my hair away from my face.

"I will never let that happen to you, little one. Daddy will always protect you." His voice is a sexy growl, sending a jolt of desire straight to my core.

Unfortunately for both of us, the alarm on Julian's watch beeps, signaling the start of his office hours.

"Saved by the bell," I breathe out.

"Oh no, little one. You're not even close to being safe. I want you in my office, on your knees next to my chair, wearing nothing but your knickers."

My mouth pops open. "What? You've got two conference calls today."

The smile spreading across his lips is pure evil. "Don't worry, love. You won't make a sound because your lips will be wrapped around my cock."

With his hands on my shoulders, he turns to me before swatting me on the behind. "Hurry along, little one. You don't want to keep Daddy waiting."

Even though Stephanie is suspicious, the excitement of Julian's plans carries me through the labyrinth of hallways until I stop in front of his office door. I run my fingers lightly over the nameplate next to the door. *Dr. Julian Armstrong*. I sigh because even though he owns me, body and soul, there's no doubt I own him.

If only he'd say it. If only he'd express his feelings for me.

I quickly unlock the door and hurry inside to undress. Sunlight streams in through the yellowed blinds on the window, warming the room, but my skin still erupts in waves of goosebumps as I undress. I place my neatly-folded clothes under my backpack, hidden from view in a corner chair, before I obediently kneel beside his chair.

The door handle slowly turns, and I feel him before I see him. The moment Julian steps inside, it's as if the air vanishes and is replaced with a thick tension. Desire and passion hang over us both as he stalks his way toward me. He says nothing as he trails his fingers along my jaw and over my bare shoulders.

He circles me like a predator until he stops right in front of me. With his hands on his hips, he spreads his legs slightly and a sharp breath escapes his lips.

"You make Daddy proud, little one," he coos. "Perfect tits made just for my hands. Gorgeous lips waiting to wrap around my cock. But you know what's really fucking sexy, little one? Your mind."

He crouches down and slips his thumb into my mouth, silently demanding me to suck it.

I don't just suck; I worship it, which earns me a gleaming smile and praise.

He withdraws his thumb and stands, backing away. His fingers are nimble as they work to unlock the metal clasp of his leather belt and then the button of his sharp black pants. He shoves his pants down his thighs and then pulls his cock, hard and proud, from his boxer briefs. My mouth waters as I wait for my taste.

"What do you want, little one?"

"Your cock," I answer.

Julian growls his disapproval, and I quickly amend my answer. "I want your cock, Daddy."

He hisses with satisfaction before he fists his cock and steps forward. He runs the tip against my lips, giving me my first taste of his saltiness. My mouth widens to accommodate his length as he settles himself against my tongue.

He draws it back before plunging it deep and hitting the back of my throat. He repeats this a few more times before unexpectedly, he withdraws and tucks his cock back inside his underwear.

I protest until he holds up a finger. "As you reminded me, I've got two conference calls to make."

Then he brushes past me and settles himself in the worn leather chair behind his desk. He spins to face me, a grin of self-satisfaction on his lips. The excitement inside me dies down until he reaches into his boxers and pulls out his cock again.

"Time to get to work, little one," he says with a waggle of his brows.

CHAPTER THIRTEEN

JULIAN

"Thank you, Michael. If you could bring those thesis proposals to me before the end of office hours today, I'll look at them. I hate to leave the students waiting for approval."

I look between my legs at Meghan's crystal blue eyes staring straight up at me. Saliva drips down the sides of her mouth as it slides up and down my cock.

Pressing the mute button on my colleagues, I address my little girl. "Such a dirty girl. Feasting on Daddy's cock while he gets work done. Just a little while longer and I'll reward you."

She pulls her mouth from me with a pop.

"Thank you, Daddy," she responds before devouring my cock again.

I stifle a groan as my engorged head hits the back of her throat. Threading my fingers through her golden locks, I reach up with the opposite hand and resume my call.

"Gentlemen, if there is nothing else, I need to get some paperwork done before my lecture starts in a few hours."

I lift my hips, shoving my cock deep into her throat. Meghan gags on my length, her eyes widening in surprise.

"Is everything all right, Julian?" Professor Herman asks. "You aren't coming down with anything, are you?"

I cough to cover Meghan's giggle. "I'm not sure. If anything, it's just a cold. Chat with you blokes next week."

Without wasting any more time, I end the call.

"Little one is being quite naughty," I growl, pulling her hair back.

Her neck stretches beautifully as she moans in both pain and pleasure.

"No more games. It's time for Daddy to fuck your mouth the way he wants. Take it like a good girl."

I stand and shove my hips forward, briefly making contact with her lips before retreating and beginning the process once again.

"Damn it, Megs. The only thing better than your mouth is your tight pussy." I pull my cock out of her mouth, hook my hands under her arms, and yank her up before slamming my mouth to hers.

She devours my soul with a single kiss. On the outside, it seems I am in control, but I'm anything but. Just as I am about to grip her under the arms and throw her on my desk, the door to my office opens.

Meghan scrambles back below my desk.

"Be quiet, little one. It seems someone has forgotten their manners," I warn her sharply before leaning forward in my chair just enough to cover myself and wait for my uninvited guest to enter.

"I'm surprised you aren't fucking her right here on your desk." Stephanie sneers as she enters my office.

"I have absolutely no idea what you're going on about," I bark, annoyed that she has once again interrupted my time.

"Where is she?" Stephanie prowls around my office, opening cabinets and closets. If I didn't know who she was looking for, I would think she was a complete nutter.

"Meghan? I would assume she's in class or on her way to one. I didn't need her today for office hours. I had conference calls, not that I need to run my schedule by you."

Leaning forward, I rest my elbows on my desk. Stephanie takes a seat in the opposite corner, and Meghan's naked form is barely concealed underneath my desk.

"You must be fucking. There can't be any other explanation for what happened this morning." Stephanie crosses her arms, pushing her ample cleavage up for me to me admire...if I wanted to.

"Explanation that I wanted nothing to do with you or what you offered me?" I reach for my teacup, but not before I feel Meghan's tiny hands wrap around my almost flaccid cock.

It seems my little one wants to play.

"Julian, we both have needs." Stephanie leans forward and wraps her hand around mine, gripping the teacup. "If you scratch my back, I'll scratch yours. This wouldn't be the first time I helped someone of your..." She pauses a moment, as if searching for the right word. "...level of expertise keep his needs in check. I am quite influential here at Danville University. I'm not someone you want as an enemy."

Meghan's lips wrap around my cock, taking me completely into her warm mouth. I use my free hand to extract Stephanie's hand from mine. Sitting back, I take a sip of tea and mask my groan of pleasure before responding to her advances.

"I don't like to repeat myself, so please don't make a habit of making me do so. I do not, nor will I ever, want my cock anywhere near your dried-up pussy, even if you were the last woman on Earth."

I reach below my desk to grip Meghan's hair as I slightly lift my hips, shoving my cock further into her mouth.

"Now, for the last time, get out of my office unless you have something to speak to me about that pertains to my work here at Danville University."

A sinister smile covers Stephanie's face before she stands and makes her way toward the door. "You had your chance, but now I'll destroy you both."

"I look forward to the challenge." Shoving my cock deeper into Meghan's mouth, I bite my lip to stifle a moan.

"Good day, Julian." She reaches for the door

before flinging it open, and it hits the wall with a thud.

"It's Dr. Armstrong, Stephanie," I call after her as her heels click down the hall.

A shrill scream of frustration can be heard shortly after.

I sigh in relief, ready to throw Meghan on the desk and have my way with her, when my colleague and friend, Samuel, appears in the doorway. "Another visit from the Danville She-Devil, I see."

"I have no idea what you saw in that woman, Samuel." I motion for him to have a seat.

"A tight pussy and a woman willing and eager to call me Daddy whenever I wanted."

Samuel and I have been friends for years after meeting at a local fetish club in London when he was a research associate at Cambridge. If he were to hear anything going on in this room, I know he'd keep it to himself.

"No pussy is worth all that aggravation, is it?" I ask, just as Meghan's head thumps on my desk.

Samuel raises his eyebrow while giving me a knowing smile. "I got what I wanted. A tenured position here at Danville, a small price to pay. Unfortunately, my friend, she has her eyes set on you. Be careful."

"So, to what do I owe the pleasure of your company?"

"I heard you were the new kid in town and wanted to see if you needed anything. But I see you're settling in just fine." He stands and heads to the door, but stops to turn back. "Is it worth the risk?"

"Every second," I respond without a thought.

CHAPTER FOURTEEN

MEGHAN

"You can come out now, little one." Julian's voice is a purr, beckoning me from my hiding spot like the Pied Piper.

There are a million questions swirling through my head, but they can all wait. Because I need to be fucked.

I slip onto Julian's desk as he approaches. He places his hands on my thighs and spreads them wide before leaning forward to bury his nose in the center of my soaked panties.

"You've been such a good girl, little one. Daddy is definitely going to reward you."

He hooks his fingers around the material and

pulls it away before taking his first taste. My entire body shudders with relief.

Thank you, Jesus.

Julian kneels, clamping his hands on my thighs and holding them firmly to the desk while he feasts. I throw my head back and moan from the warmth of his tongue against my aching folds. He sucks my clit sharply between his lips and lets it pop out, eliciting a whimper from the back of my throat.

I collapse onto the ancient wooden top as my body writhes. My hips buck, pressing my pussy against his lips. His only reaction is to tighten his grip on me. My first orgasm builds quickly until I'm panting and begging.

"Please, Daddy. Oh, please."

He chuckles and pulls away. "Oh, no. You're going to come all over my cock."

In one fluid motion, he shoves his trousers down and pulls out his hard cock. He runs his hand over the leaking tip and then lines it up with my waiting entrance. He says nothing. He simply plunges himself deep inside me, all the way to the root.

"Christ, Meghan," he grits out. "Your pussy is always so tight. Like it was made for me."

I reach up and run my hand down the side of his cheek. "It is, Daddy. Just for you."

There's no working up to the frantic and punishing pace Julian sets as he pulls all the way out before slamming back into me. We've both been so worked up, waiting for this moment, enduring countless interruptions, and now we deserve to just explode.

Over and over, he sinks deeply into me until a familiar tension works its way through me. Sweat from Julian's forehead drips down onto my bare chest as he shakes. The battle to remain in control is written all over his face.

"Let go," I encourage him as I follow my advice.

The uncomfortable hardness pressing against my back dissolves to a dull ache. The almost painful grip Julian has on my hips as he keeps me pinned down disappears.

All that exists is us. I've never felt more connected to him.

A low rumble builds in his chest until he roars through his climax, spilling into me. I'm right there with him, gritting my teeth because I want to scream. I whisper my encouragement because I want him to fill me, to mark me. I am his forever.

He collapses on top of me, his large body

covering mine as his hands slip around my back and cradle me.

"I love you, little one," he says so softly I barely hear him. "I'll protect you, I promise."

He lifts his head to look at me. His eyes are dark and serious, but I'm not sure how I feel. I've dreamed of this moment for so long.

"Say it again," I urge him.

"I love you, Meghan," he repeats.

This time, I can't hold back the tears. They slip down my cheeks, and Julian is there, fluttering soft kisses across my face as he repeats himself over and over.

"Say you're mine," he urges me, running his hand through my hair.

"Of course, I'm yours! I'll always be yours," I tell him. "I love you."

I feel him harden inside me again and we move slowly together. My body aches and protests, but I don't care. He holds me firmly against him as he drives deep into me again.

"That's it, little one. Show Daddy how much you love him."

A gasp escapes my lips as his mouth clamps down on my bare breast, tugging the nipple with his teeth. His hand snakes between our bodies and down to my core, and his fingers lightly brush against my clit. I shudder with delight and beg him for more.

"Tremble for Daddy," he encourages me with a whisper in my ear.

I writhe against him as his fingers play my body masterfully. He strums and strokes my clit, knowing when to give me more and when to pull back, purposefully keeping me right on the edge.

"Let me come," I beg breathlessly.

But my pleas fall on deaf ears.

"You know better than that, little one," he admonishes me as he plunges himself deep inside me.

My head falls back, and I grasp Julian's arms.

"Please let me come, Daddy," I moan.

With one arm wrapped tightly around my middle, he rolls to his back and pulls me on top of him.

"Make yourself come," he commands me. "Make my cock fill your pussy."

Slowly, I rock against him, rolling my hips until need overtakes all sensibility and I lose control. I bounce up and down on his cock and reach up to cup my breasts, grabbing them and pinching the nipples. He hisses his appreciation for what I assume must be one hell of a show.

His hands are firm on my legs, holding them in place while I fuck him. I succumb to the savageness of my own needs and finally, just take.

Take the pleasure he is offering me with his body.

Take the love he is finally giving to me.

Take the desire that fills me.

And finally. I take my own bliss.

"Oh, Daddy," I moan out, closing my eyes as my orgasm barrels through me.

We both tremble through powerful climaxes as his cock pulses against my walls. My hips move in slow circles, milking everything from him until we both sigh.

My eyes flutter open and I look around the office as a grin slowly spreads across my lips. From the corner of my eye, I catch a shadow pass by the window in Julian's door. It's covered with a set of ancient mini blinds that have been drawn tight, but then I glance down at the lock.

"Julian," I say, with urgency rising in my voice.

"Tsk, tsk, little one," he chides me, but I don't care about being his little one right now.

"Julian, listen to me," I hiss. "You didn't lock the door!"

Julian bolts up, practically knocking me off his lap, and turns to face the door. "Fuck!"

"I thought I saw someone outside."

His face is calm as he faces me. "Relax, Megs. I'm sure it was only the sun or something. Why would anyone come down here? Stephanie stuck me all the way in bloody Antarctica."

"But what if she came back? You heard her, Julian. She's dead set on ruining us both."

He wraps his hands around my head and kisses me firmly. "Don't worry, little one. After the dressing down I gave her, I hardly think she'd come back today."

But it's hard to find comfort in his words with the heavy pit settling in my stomach. Something isn't right. I know what I saw, but only time will tell if I'm right.

CHAPTER FIFTEEN

JULIAN

One would assume things would become easier for Meghan and I once we told each other how we felt, but in our case, it was the exact opposite. Whatever Meghan saw outside my office door transformed her into a ball of nerves. She refused to come to my office hours or spend any time with me outside of my flat in the converted Victorian.

Not that there has been much time for anything other than sleeping. With the winter break approaching, students are eager to turn in final projects, which means my office hours are being used for their intended purpose. I'm also buried up to my neck in grading, which only adds to my stress.

"What?" I growl toward the unexpected visitor entering my office.

It's late, and Meghan has yet again refused a quick nosh with me between classes.

"Someone seems to be in a bad mood." Samuel strolls in and takes a seat on the other side of the desk.

"Bad mood doesn't even cover how I feel." I lean back in my chair and cross my arms over my chest.

"Is Daddy pouting?" Samuel pushes his chair back a few inches, no doubt in response to the low rumbling growl that leaves my lips.

"First, never, and I mean *never*, call me Daddy again. Second, I don't pout. I just miss her." I turn to my left and look at the space on the shelf I made for Meghan to keep books and snacks when she comes to visit.

"Well, well. Someone has tamed the savage beast. I never thought I would live to see that day."

"Stop gloating and help me figure things out. She's paranoid that something will happen." I sigh, deciding whether I want to tell him everything.

"I can't help if I don't know the entire story." Samuel waits patiently for me to make my decision.

I push back from my desk, stand from the chair,

and start talking. I tell him how we met at Cambridge, how I knew I loved her the moment she spilled scalding hot tea in my lap, and how I came all the way to America to find her.

Pacing my office, I tell him about the complications with Stephanie and her desire to ruin Meghan's chance at graduation. Samuel sits there the entire time, listening to my tale, never once interrupting me. Admittedly, it feels good to get some of this off my chest. And the more I reveal, the lighter I feel.

"Now you know everything. What do we do?" I sink back into my chair, resting my head on the desk.

I'm worn out, feeling completely defeated. I'm supposed to protect her from everything, but right now, it's clear she is trying to protect me.

"My friend, you are good and fucked."

I reach into the top desk drawer and pull out an old, worn packet of cigarettes. I haven't smoked in years, a filthy habit I picked up during my undergrad years to help relieve some of the tension and get me through late nights. But right now, I'm craving old habits.

"Put that away. We just need to think for a moment. You're more worried about losing her than anything. Am I wrong?" Samuel rests his arm on the edge of the desk.

"Yes. I'll do anything to keep her with me forever," I answer without hesitation.

There is nothing I wouldn't do to ensure Meghan remains safe and in my arms for the rest of our lives.

"Then you have two options: continue to wait for whatever Stephanie has in store for both of you or accept the fact that she has something up her sleeve and bring her down once she plays her hand."

"What do you think she's playing at, Samuel?"

"If I know anything about Stephanie, it's that she is vain. She does not take kindly to being insulted. You not falling at her feet is an insult. She is prepared to do anything."

Maybe Meghan isn't being so paranoid after all, but I need to have my girl securely in my arms. We both need it; the strain of this predicament is wearing on both of us.

"Thanks, mate. I appreciate it. I think both of us need to get away. My mum has been pestering me about coming home for the holidays. I think this is the perfect time for Meghan to meet her."

"Are you sure she is ready to take such a huge step?"

The questioning look in Samuel's eyes has me wondering the same thing. Meghan and I are still very much in the early stages of our relationship. Personal details like family are rarely discussed. But still…

"She's mine. What better way to show her how much she means to me than to introduce her to my mum over the holidays?"

Samuel stands and comes around to stand beside me. I look up, meeting my friend's stare. I'm surprised to find understanding and even envy in his eyes, but before I can say anything, he pats my shoulder and turns to leave.

"You'll find her someday, Samuel. Probably when you least expect it."

"Someday is already here, my friend." Samuel gives me a sad smile before leaving me to my thoughts.

I flip open my laptop and begin planning. Meghan may avoid spending time with me on campus, but she won't have any excuse when there's an ocean between us and Stephanie.

CHAPTER SIXTEEN

MEGHAN

I am a bitch to be around at the end of the semester.

"Meghan!" Julian shouts from the small kitchen in his apartment. "What in the bloody hell is this?"

I feel like a slug as I make my way slowly to the kitchen. I stayed up far too late last night working on an essay for my feminist literature class. Not even the sight of Julian with his tortoiseshell glasses perched on his nose can energize me.

He's standing in front of an impressive array of Styrofoam containers, the remnants of last night's instant noodle feast.

"I'll clean it up," I tell him with little enthusiasm. "It was a late night."

"And what's this?" He uses his toe to press down on the lever that opens the lid of the trash can, revealing more of my nasty end-of-semester habits.

Empty boxes and bags from my favorite doughnut place are right on top, but buried beneath those are cookie boxes.

I roll my eyes because having to explain myself is exhausting. "Sorry. I had an exam at eight this morning and I only got like two hours of sleep. Sugar is life, Jules."

"What the fuck?"

I turn to leave, but the growl in his voice stops me dead in my tracks. Well, shit. I've poked the bear.

"Living room. *Now*."

He marches past me and into the next room, where he sits down on the leather sofa. His expression is stern, and all it takes is one look to understand his intention.

I'm getting spanked.

"You know what to do by now, little one." His voice is a purr, but it's firm.

My feet carry me automatically toward him, and I drape myself over his knee. His hands are warm as they slip under the waistband of my yoga pants before tugging them, and my panties, down.

He sucks in a sharp breath. Oh, yeah. I'm also wearing my ugliest pair of granny panties.

Without preamble, his hand comes down sharply on my ass. It stings, but fuck, does it feel good.

"That's for calling me 'Jules.' Never do that again."

"Yes, Daddy," I murmur.

His hand lands another blow. "And that's for wearing these awful knickers. When we're finished, you're going to throw away every godforsaken pair. I'll buy you new ones much more suitable."

"Yes, Daddy," I reply.

This punishment continues a little while longer. An infraction follows each searing smack. But this is a much-needed reminder that I belong to him. He owns me, and during the pressure of these last few weeks, I've gotten too comfortable.

By the time he's finished, I'm wet and needy, squirming on his lap. Should I beg him for release? God knows we both need it. Or should I accept my unfulfilled desire as a part of my punishment?

Julian decides for me. "Up on the couch, little one. Daddy only has time for a quick fuck before his lecture."

He's hard and relentless as he drives his cock

into me, filling me deeply, stretching my walls. I groan every time he buries himself and his balls slap against my sensitive folds. When his thumb presses against the one area we've yet to explore, I moan.

"Mmm. Does my little one want her Daddy to claim her ass?" There's a sound of delight in his voice.

Now I know what to get him for Christmas.

"Oh yes, Daddy," I answer.

He presses his thumb inside the tight, puckered hole a little more, and I scream. He hisses with pleasure and praises me.

"I'm going to fill you up, little one," he grunts out as his cock pulses inside me. "And you're going to attend class with my cum dripping down your thighs. No knickers allowed."

He surges inside of me one final time, pushing me right into my orgasm. Julian reaches around, and his fingers bury themselves in my folds, teasing another orgasm from me until I'm a quivering mess.

I feel him harden inside me, but unexpectedly, he pulls out.

"Daddy can't be late, little one. Tonight, I'm going to fuck you properly."

But plans change.

Like a good girl, I obey Julian and head to campus with a damp pair of yoga pants. A secret smile plays on my lips as I head to the library. Having him punish and dominate me energized me and cleared away some of the fogginess of the past few weeks.

"Well, don't you look like the cat who ate the canary?" Stephanie's voice puts a damper on my mood.

Fuck. I'd forgotten all about her. I brushed off our last meeting, faking illness, and our only correspondence since has been through email.

"Hi, Stephanie," I greet her. "Wasn't expecting to see you."

Her lips form a tight line. "I bet. Since you can't be bothered to show up to our meetings, I guess I have to deliver the bad news myself. I'm rejecting your capstone project."

"You can't do that! It's the end of the semester!"

"Your research into Desdemona is like another well-known Shakespeare scholar. You know Danville's policy on plagiarism."

Unshed tears sting my eyes. I will not cry in front of this bitch.

"Are you kidding me? The research is entirely

my own! How can you reject it again? I won't graduate!"

She pouts her lips. "That's too bad, *Megs*."

Then she brushes past me and walks away without another word.

My eyes widen with horror.

She knows!

I race toward the building where Julian's class is located. That bitch fucking knows about us. I clamber up the stairs of the building and hurry inside before locating the lecture hall. Without a second thought, I burst through the door and Julian stops his lecture.

"I'm so sorry," I whisper. "But this is an emergency."

Julian excuses himself and quickly walks toward me.

"What is it?" he asks through gritted teeth.

"Stephanie knows about us," I hiss. "She just stopped me outside the library to tell me my capstone project was rejected."

"Bitch," Julian mutters. "But that doesn't mean she knows anything."

"She called me 'Megs.' You're the only one who calls me that! How else would she know?"

He places a firm hand on my arm and looks me

dead in the eye. "There is absolutely no way she knows. I promise. Now, go back to my flat, take a hot bath, and relax. We'll figure out a solution to this nightmare."

I nod. I have one more exam, but I currently have an A in the class, so if I skip it, it won't really affect my grade.

"Okay," I breathe.

He closes the door to the lecture hall before pulling me into his arms. It's a risk to show me any kind of affection outside his office or flat, but I sink into his embrace without much care.

Let them see, I think.

"Everything will be okay, little one," he whispers, then kisses the top of my head. "I love you."

When Julian returns home a few hours later, I'm slightly calmer, but not much. I couldn't care less about Stephanie knowing about my relationship with Julian. I'm an adult and our relationship began outside Danville University. But ruining my chance at graduation? That makes me freak the fuck out.

The moment Julian steps through the front door, I pounce, assaulting him with questions.

"What am I going to do, Julian? The semester is over, and I have no capstone project! I've worked so hard for this and she's ruining everything! Why is she doing this to us? To me?"

He grips my shoulders. "Settle down, Megs. Come on, let's have a seat. I've got a few things to tell you."

Unexpectedly, tears fall down my cheeks and a heavy pit settles in my stomach. "Are you ending this? Are we over? Oh, God. I can't lose you too!"

He chuckles as he leads me over to the couch. "You're so fucking gorgeous when you're hysterical."

We settle onto the couch, and he pulls me into the warmth of his embrace.

"First, you're mine. *Forever*."

I sigh with relief.

"I'm sorry," I whisper. "I'm so tired and stressed."

He brushes my hair back from my face. "I know, love. And that's why I'm taking you away on holiday."

CHAPTER SEVENTEEN

JULIAN

I cradle Meghan in my lap as I continue to explain my plan. "My mum has been begging me to come home for the holidays. Originally, I was going to stay here with you. However, considering recent events, I think we both need to get away from Danville."

Meghan looks up at me, her eyes filled with unshed tears.

"Why?" she whispers.

"Because it's my job to take care of you, little one, but more importantly, because I love you. You're my world." I brush a gentle kiss on her forehead

Meghan has no real family to speak of. Her parents both died in a car accident when she was in her teens, and her elderly grandmother is in a nursing home. She usually spends her breaks here on campus working on schoolwork. With graduation approaching, I assumed she would want to remain here.

Now that I think about it, we never discussed our holiday plans.

"Did you have other plans for the holiday break?" I reach back and rub my neck, nervous to hear her response.

"Of course not. There's nowhere I'd rather be than with you." She flings her arms around my neck, bringing her petite body closer to mine.

"Then it's settled. I phoned my mum and told her to expect us. We leave tomorrow morning; I already booked our tickets."

"What would you have done if I said no?" She leans back and gives me a questioning look.

"Spanked you until you gave me the answer I wanted. Are you allowed to tell me no, little one?"

"No, Daddy," she answers with a seductive smile, then bites down on her bottom lip and looks up at me through her lashes. "Would you like your Christmas present early?"

My cock hardens against my trousers. I can't imagine what she'd give me, but from the naughty gleam in her eye, there's no doubt I'm going to enjoy it.

"Hurry, Megs, or we'll miss our flight!" I yell down the hall for the third time before checking my watch.

The car has arrived to take us to the airport, but Meghan is still in the bedroom, double and triple checking to make sure she doesn't leave anything behind.

As I'm about to yell for a fourth time, she comes barreling down the hall.

"Sorry! I wanted to make sure I wasn't forgetting anything. I usually have more than a few hours to pack." She rushes past me as I reach down and give her bottom a swat.

"If you hadn't teased me with my Christmas present while we were packing, you would have had plenty of time to pack."

My mind drifts to the scraps of lingerie scattered across my bedroom floor, mere gift wrap for the real present Meghan gave me: her arse. We started slowly, with just a little silver plug I worked into her tightly puckered hole as I fucked her. She assumed I'd take her arse with my cock, but I'm saving that for Christmas morning. Fantasies of fucking her in front of the tree and roaring fire dance in my thoughts like naughty little sugar plums.

Merry old England, here we come, I think to myself as I lock the door to my flat.

The trip to the airport is uneventful and we arrive with plenty of time to make it through security and grab something to eat.

"I need coffee ASAP. I'm dead on my feet," Meghan whines as we trudge through the crowd.

I want to scold her; after all, she's part of the reason we only had a few hours to pack and sleep. I shoot her a stern look, and a blush color covers her cheeks.

"You'll have plenty of time to sleep on the plane," I admonish her before pressing a gentle kiss on her forehead.

I spot a coffee shop and guide her toward it. I booked us first-class tickets, so we should receive a full breakfast, but something to nosh on before then won't hurt.

Just as our names are called for our order, an unexpected visitor arrives.

"Dr. Armstrong, what a surprise! I thought you

were staying in town for the holiday break?" Stephanie greets us both with a warm smile that almost seems genuine.

"That was the plan, but my mum called and begged me to come home. Can't say no to mum." I plaster on a fake smile and wait for the claws to come out.

"And Meghan, are you going to visit your grandmother?" She turns her attention to my little one, who trembles beside me.

"Yes, I am. Dr. Armstrong was kind enough to give me a ride to the airport," she explains.

"And now he's buying you breakfast? How sweet."

"Just a little gift for all her hard work this semester," I reply.

"Well, I will leave you two to catch your flights. Enjoy your holiday and have a great break." With a smile and a wave, Stephanie disappears into the crowd of holiday travelers.

"See, little one? There's nothing to worry about. She was at least pleasant this time. She has no idea what's going on. Even assumed you were going home and not somewhere with me." I smile down at her, but her face is anything but relaxed.

"I know what I heard. She knows about us. I

don't know what she's playing at right now, but she *is* up to something," Meghan growls at me before storming toward our gate.

She has been under so much stress recently and she is tired, so I let her tantrum slide. But if she doesn't get herself sorted by the time we get to my mum's, she will have one sore arse.

Once I arrive at our gate, Meghan is seated in front of the wall of windows overlooking the tarmac.

"Is this seat taken?" I ask politely before easing myself into the spot next to her. "Little one, I will not hesitate to pull your knickers down and spank your delicious bottom in front of all these nice people."

She stares at me, wide-eyed with defiance. "She doesn't have me fooled, Julian."

I reach over and pat her thigh.

"Let Daddy take care of this," I murmur in her ear. "Trust me."

She shivers and squirms, a sign that my job is done.

"Unless of course, you want to be punished."

CHAPTER EIGHTEEN

MEGHAN

W hen Julian goes into full Daddy mode, something inside me ignites. It's like an involuntary reaction. But I also know I'm right. I don't buy Stephanie's polite-as-fuck act for a minute. I'll be on high alert from now until I've got my diploma firmly in hand.

"There is something I want to talk to you about," Julian says coolly as he pulls away and crosses one long leg over the other. "When we get back, I think you should file a complaint against Stephanie."

"You're joking, right?" Inside, I'm screaming, because moments ago, he was telling me I had nothing to worry about.

"No, I'm not. Even though I don't think she

suspects anything, she also isn't behaving in your best interest as your advisor. It's borderline academic negligence."

"I don't want to poke the bear, Julian. I've already emailed Dr. Nelson and asked him if he'll consider taking me on. I sent him the project proposal we worked on together. I know the claim of plagiarism is bogus, so I don't think he'll have a problem with the topic, but he rarely takes undergrads."

Julian hums. "Well, we'll wait to see what he says. But if he turns down your offer, we're going to file a complaint. Don't fight me, little one."

I tentatively agree with his plan. We finish our coffee and snack just as our flight is called. When they call for first-class passengers, Julian stands.

"That's us," he says casually. "Let's go."

I'm stunned as I reach for his hand, and he practically drags me down the jetway and onto the plane.

"Th-this is too much," I stammer. "You shouldn't have spent all this money on me."

Julian takes my carry-on from me and slides it into the space above our seats. When he turns back toward me, he grasps my chin firmly between his thumb and forefinger.

"Nonsense. Megs, you deserve this. Let me spoil you."

He kisses me soundly, ending all discussion on this matter. I want to ask him how he can possibly afford two first-class seats on a professor's salary, but he shuts down any questions with a dark gleam in his eye.

"It's a long flight, little one. I want to relax and enjoy it, because the moment we land in London, I've got plans for you. Save your strength."

Julian's word is final, and any petulant thoughts I had disappear. Not long into the flight, the attendant comes around and offers to help us convert our seats into beds. Taking a nap isn't a bad idea. I've had so little sleep over the last few weeks, and once I stretch out, I find it easy to drift off.

I wake up just before we begin our descent into London. Julian is still stretched out in his converted bed, but he's awake.

"How long will it take to get to your mother's cottage?"

His voice is soft and low as he answers. "About two hours, maybe a little longer." He reaches across to brush his fingers across my cheek. "How was your nap?"

"Good. I've never slept so well on a flight before."

He smiles brightly. "One perk of flying first class."

"Thank you, Julian. It was a lovely surprise."

His fingers trail lightly along my jaw and then down my neck. "I love you, Meghan. I want you to know that. I've never loved anyone so fiercely before."

I lean into his touch. "I love you, too, Julian. You've given me back something that's been missing for a long time."

"And what's that, little one?"

I hesitate before I answer. Telling him I love him is one thing, but telling him I feel so much more is daunting. When I think about my future, I can easily picture him there with me. We fit so perfectly together, in and out of the bedroom. But I have no idea if he has similar thoughts.

"Safety. Security. Family."

Before he can respond, the pilot announces our final descent into London and the flight attendants help return our seats to their proper position. I don't press him further, because if he sees me in his future, he'll tell me.

When we arrive in London, there's a lot of hurry

up and wait. We rush to customs, only to wait for what seems like hours. Then we wait for our luggage, and finally the rental car. But I can't stop thinking about Julian's delicious warning: once we arrive in London, he's got plans.

"Are we going right to your mother's cottage?" I ask him as we settle into the luxury sedan he's rented.

"Yes, sort of. We're staying in a separate cottage on the property."

"And will we see her tonight?"

He turns and shoots me a Cheshire cat grin. "Eager to get me alone, little one?"

I can't stop the blush from creeping up my cheeks. "Don't you want the rest of your Christmas present?"

"I'm quite keen for the rest of it, actually. Doesn't mean I haven't got my own plans for you."

I press my thighs together to relieve the ache that's been growing inside me. Sometimes, I don't feel whole without Julian's domination. My Daddy is what's held me together these last few weeks. Submitting to him every night gave me the strength to face Stephanie and to power through the grueling finals and essays.

Cookies also helped. But mostly, it was Julian.

Being back in England with him almost seems surreal. We make small talk as we drive along the highway. He tells me he'll take me to Stratford-upon-Avon and Oxford, which is exciting, but honestly, I'm content to just be with him freely. There's no sneaking around or hiding. We can be ourselves and be together without risking someone reporting him to the Board of Directors.

"Do you have any brothers or sisters?" I ask casually.

"Only child, I'm afraid. Which means my mum might be a tad unbearable when we arrive," he explains.

"Overprotective?" I guess.

"No, overeager. I haven't brought many women home to meet her."

"Oh." I don't know why that surprises me. Maybe because it's still so hard for me to believe a man like Julian hasn't been claimed by another woman. "Why me?"

"Don't you know, little one? You're mine, *forever*."

CHAPTER NINETEEN

JULIAN

During the drive, Meghan peppers me with questions about my mother and my time growing up.

"Are we almost there?" She fidgets in her seat, her head swiveling as she takes in the scenery around us as it changes from the city-like skyline to the rural countryside I grew up in.

"There's nothing for you to be nervous about, little one. My mum is going to love you." I reach over and grab her hand, giving it a light squeeze. "We should arrive in about fifteen minutes. My mum doesn't live too far outside the city."

Meghan bites her bottom lip, bringing a growl from my lips.

"You'd better let that lip go right this minute. Otherwise, I'll pull off the road and have my way with you."

With a giggle, she releases her lip. "Sorry."

"That's better. Now, relax. Everything will be fine. My mum will probably have made her famous lamb stew for dinner, but we've had such a long day of travel, we can excuse ourselves to bed early. Not that I plan on letting you go directly to sleep."

Meghan grins with approval before turning back to the window. It only takes us another few minutes before we pull down the winding drive toward my mother's cottage.

"Julian, it's beautiful!" Her nose is pushed up against the window as she takes in the lush scenery.

"You should see it when the sun is high. There is an apple orchard just a little to the south of here. I'll take you into the village for apple cider if you're good."

The house is just as I remember it, not that I've been gone for long. Surrounded by nothing but greenery, the all-brick, one-story cottage has been my home all my life. There's a small patio on the side of the house with a table and chairs and double sets of French doors that lead into the main living area. Smoke billows from the chimney, which means my mum has lit a fire in anticipation of our arrival.

I park the car in the drive and turn to Meghan, whose eyes are as big as saucers.

"What's that look for, little one?"

"How did you even fit in there?"

I let out a boisterous laugh. "I wasn't always this big. Besides, it goes back quite a way into the forest. The front is mainly the family room, kitchen and dining room."

I press a gentle kiss to her forehead before opening the car door to get our bags. The moment I step out, I hear the warble of my mother's voice.

"There's my precious boy. Hurry and get your arse in here. I had to beg you to come home. Now you're makin' me wait on you."

Meghan's laughter catches the attention of my mother, who gives her a once over.

"Let me get a good look at you."

She heads right toward Meghan, reaching out to give her a motherly hug. The two of them look thick as thieves as they melt into each other's arms.

"Thank you for inviting me into your home, Mrs. Armstrong."

"None of that Mrs. Armstrong nonsense. Call me Sara. Or better yet, call me Mum."

I roll my eyes because I was afraid of this. Mum's been pestering me about settling down since the moment I left university.

"Now, let me get you inside. Apparently my son forgot his manners."

After getting the evil eye from her, I follow the two of them inside.

"You must be starved! I'll fix you a bite to eat, sweetheart. You're damn near skin and bones." Mum clicks her tongue at me. "Go take those bags to the cottage in the back. You need to light the fire as well."

Before heading to the cottage, I leave a lingering kiss on Meghan's cheek.

"Behave yourself," I whisper.

"I make no promises."

"The cheek," I playfully scold her before leaving out the back door.

The cottage behind the house is a lot smaller than our home, but it will be perfect for us during our short stay here. It used to be my dad's old work-shop, but after he passed, I helped convert it into a guest house. Now my mum doesn't have to worry about having space when people come to visit.

Mum has already made the bed and placed fresh towels in the small half-bathroom. We won't be able to shower in here. The plumbing isn't quite as it should be, but we will be able to get cleaned up after our evening activities.

I drop our bags and head out to the side of the house and grab an armful of wood. All it takes is a few logs to get the fire burning. Once the fire warms the small space, I return to the main house.

Meghan's laughter mixed with my mum's is the first thing I hear.

"What's so funny?"

"Sara was telling me stories about you when you were a boy."

Mum scowls, giving her a gentle slap on her hand before getting up and heading toward the kitchen. "What did I tell you about calling me Sara? It's *Mum*."

I pull out the chair next to Meghan, leaning down to whisper in her ear. "I told you she would adore you."

"No funny business at my table. Now, you two eat."

I can't help but chuckle at my mother before digging into my food.

Dinner goes by with quiet conversation. Mum

asks the general get-to-know-you questions, smothering Meghan in motherly love once she tells her about the loss of her parents.

"Hopefully, I'll be calling you my daughter sooner rather than later." Mum shoots me a look before grabbing our plates and taking them to the kitchen.

"We aren't rushing into anything right now. Meghan is finishing her degree. She has her whole future ahead of her." I turn and smile at Meghan, who looks stricken. I reach out and run a hand down her arm. "Are you all right?"

Meghan's face transforms instantly into a smile that seems forced. "I'm fine. Long day is all."

I don't buy Meghan's excuse for a second, but I let it slide for now. I gather up the remaining dishes from the table and take them to the sink. If I know my mother, the next thing she'll be asking about is children. I don't want Meghan to think I'm trying to impede her dreams for the future.

"And don't start asking for grandbabies either. We will get to all these things in time, but not anytime soon."

Meghan pushes her chair back and stands. "Thank you for the lovely dinner, but I didn't realize how tired I was. If you'll excuse me, I'm going to head to bed."

"Of course, child. Just head straight out the back and down the path. You can't miss it."

I stand to follow her, but she holds out her hand to stop me.

"You should stay. Catch up with your mom. I'll be fine."

I hear a touch of disappointment in her voice. With all the chaos of the semester, we haven't really talked much about our future together. Without a doubt, Meghan is mine and eventually we will marry, but it's not important now. I've long thought Meghan felt the same way, but from the pained look on her face, I was wrong.

"Well, son. You stuck your foot in it, running your mouth this time. Just how do you plan to rectify the situation?"

"I don't know what you mean."

My mum nods her head toward the back of the house. "That girl wants to marry you, and you just dashed her dreams."

"I did no such thing."

She scoffs. "Son, you might have a bunch of fancy degrees, but clearly, you've lost a bit of common sense."

I lean back in my chair and drum my fingers on the kitchen table.

My mum pats me on the shoulder. "I'll put on the kettle on, and we'll have a long chat."

CHAPTER TWENTY

MEGHAN

I feel like an idiot. When Julian said he was taking me home to meet his mother, I assumed…

Well, there's the problem. I assumed. Julian's words ring loudly in my ears, and I can't help but wonder if I'm truly his. If forever with Julian is no longer an option, then why even bring me here?

I swipe at the stupid tears trickling down my cheeks. It's not as if we've talked long-term commitment. We've been far too busy battling Stephanie and finishing the semester to talk about anything beyond the end of the academic year.

I head to the small bathroom and wipe off some of the travel grime. Sometimes washing up with hot, soapy water makes things clearer, but when I look at my freshly scrubbed face in the mirror, I still feel confused.

What kind of future does Julian picture for us?

The front door to the cottage opens, signaling his return, and I step out of the bathroom as he enters the living room.

"I think we should have a talk," he says sternly.

"Are you mad?" I ask.

His tone confuses me and I'm not sure what I did to deserve his anger.

"More so at myself than at you, little one." He sits down on the small sofa and pats the space beside him. "Come on, Megs. Let's have a chat."

There's a bit of awkward silence as I settle myself next to him. It's almost laughable, two grown adults who have no idea how to have a conversation about the future.

"I know we've never really talked about it—"

I cut him off. "Do you want to marry me or not?"

His mouth opens slightly, but I'm not quite finished.

"Because if you don't, then why bring me all the way here?"

"Meghan, you're only twenty-one."

"So? What does my age have to do with anything?"

"You've barely lived a life, little one. As much as I want to show you the world, I don't want to deprive you of it, either."

"You're not depriving me of anything. I know exactly what I want, Julian." My heart pounds and I push to my feet. "I knew when I was little that I wanted to study Shakespeare. And I know I want to marry you and have your children."

Julian's eyes widen slightly. "Let's not talk about children yet."

"Then maybe we should be more careful," I hiss.

There are no barriers between Julian and me. The only thing preventing pregnancy is the tiny pink pill I take faithfully every morning. But Julian's healthy appetite sometimes makes me wonder if we're walking a fine line.

Julian stands and grips my arm firmly but not painfully. "Let's get one thing clear, little one. I will have you whenever wherever I want. I could bend you over this sofa right now and fuck you."

"Then do it," I challenge him.

Regretfully, he lets go of my arm. "No. We have far more important things to discuss. But challenge me again and I'll make your arse so red you won't be able to sit for days."

"I just want to know if there's a future for us, Julian. That's all."

He pinches the bridge of his nose. "I'm not a goddamn fortune teller, Meghan."

I can't help the way I feel. I ache with disappointment.

"Oh, I see."

"Do you want a ring? Is that what this is all about? Shall I head back to London and pick you out a great, glittering diamond for your finger?"

"No! That's not what I want."

Not yet anyway.

"Then tell me, Meghan, because I'm fucking clueless. One minute, you think Stephanie is after us, and the next, you went to head down to the church."

"That's not what I'm saying, Julian. When you say I'm yours 'forever,' what does that mean? Until the end of the semester? The end of the year? Because to me, forever means until the end of time."

He runs his hands through his dark hair. "I can't tell you that, Meghan."

My shoulders sag. "Then I shouldn't be here."

I look around the room and spot my suitcase, which is still packed. It's going to cost a pretty penny to get a flight back to the States on such short notice, but I can't stay here.

"What? You want to leave?"

I nod, willing myself not to cry. If I cry, I'm going to give in and stay and let him Daddy mind-fuck me.

"Yes, I do. I know what I want, Julian, but I don't think you do."

"If that's what you want, then I'll take you back to London in the morning."

There's no further discussion or argument.

We move silently around the cottage, but I can't stand the thought of sleeping in the same bed with him. I search the room for some place to sleep and my eyes land on the sofa. It's small and not as comfortable as a bed, but at least I'll be warm.

Pulling the heavy throw off the end of the bed, I grab a pillow and head toward the couch.

"Where do you think you're going?" Julian asks.

"To bed," I respond.

Did he honestly think I would sleep in the bed with him as if nothing happened?

"I will not let you sleep on that thing all night.

I'll sleep in my old room tonight and come back in the morning to take you to the airport."

I watch as he slips on his jeans and coat before heading into the bedroom. His heavy footsteps echo in the cottage as he moves around the living space. My entire body is tense under the duvet as I wait for the sound of the door opening and closing.

Instead, the sound of Julian's footsteps gets closer until he appears in the doorway of the bedroom. He approaches me slowly, his expression impassive.

"Good night, little one." He gently kisses my forehead before he turns to leave.

I breathe a heavy sigh of relief and sink into the bed, hoping for a decent night's sleep.

In the morning, Julian places my luggage in the trunk and we drive in near silence back to London. He holds my hand the entire way.

When we arrive at Heathrow, Julian surprises me with a plane ticket.

"I hope you don't mind, but I bought you a ticket. I'm afraid it's not first class, though."

"Thank you," I tell him.

We stand on the sidewalk staring at each other for a long while until, at last, he leans forward and brushes a kiss against my cheek.

"Have a safe trip back."

Nothing else is said between us. I can't bring myself to watch him drive away, so I busy myself with checking in for my flight. I let the chaotic atmosphere of the airport consume me, because if I bother to stop for a moment and truly think about what I just did, then tears would start and never stop.

CHAPTER TWENTY-ONE

JULIAN

"What have you done now, son?" Mum is waiting for me as I head into the kitchen after dropping Meghan off at the airport.

This is not how imagined this visit going. I wanted to give her a nice holiday. A chance for us to reconnect after all the stress we have both been under with the threats from Stephanie and finals hanging over our heads. Instead, my mouth ruined everything.

"Good morning, Mum."

I drop the keys to the rental car on the table and give her a kiss on the cheek before having a seat at the table.

"What's for breakfast? I'm starving." I try to

add fake enthusiasm into my voice, hoping my mum won't ask questions.

No matter what I do, she'll know something is up.

"Why would you bring such a sweet girl like that home with you only to cock things up?" She smacks me on the back of the head like she did when I was a child.

"Bloody hell, Mum! What was that for?"

"That's for getting up the hopes of an old lady! I want to see you settled, Julian. I want to be a Nan!" She smacks me again. "And that's for Meghan. Poor girl."

Memories of Meghan flash through my mind.

"I ruined everything. I couldn't promise her forever."

"And why the fuck not?"

I reel back in shock. I've only heard my mother swear a handful of times, but every time is just as surprising.

"Mum, *language*."

"Don't be such a prude. I only curse when it's necessary. Right now, it's necessary. Why did you bring her here if you weren't ready to promise her your heart?"

I open my mouth to respond, but close it immediately. Why *did* I bring Meghan here? I wanted to get her away from everything going on at Danville, but more importantly, I wanted her to meet my mother.

I wanted my little one to know where I came from.

I wanted her to know the type of man I am outside the university.

I wanted her to know what forever would be like.

"I wanted to show her what life with me would be like, but she has her whole life ahead of her." I reach back and rub my neck as my conversation with Meghan last night fills my mind. "I don't want to promise her anything I can't give."

She takes a seat next to me and wraps her small hand around mine. "It's all right to be afraid. Forever is a strong word. It's a promise you'll love and cherish someone until the end of time. Is that something you're prepared to do for Meghan?"

I don't even have to think about my answer. "Yes."

I love Meghan with everything I am. I will do anything for her, even let her go.

"Does she feel the same way about you?"

"I…I don't know."

"Have you asked her?" She gives my hand a gentle squeeze.

I never even bothered to ask Meghan what she wants. Maybe this *is* her forever. Finishing her degree and coming back to England to live in a tiny cottage.

She might not want to spread her wings or see the rest of the world. If she does, who says we can't do it together?

"I'm an idiot." I look at my mum, who has a beautiful smile on her face and unshed tears collecting in her eyes.

"Yes, you are. Now, what are you going to do about it?"

"I'm going to stop sitting here and feeling sorry for myself and get her back. But first, I plan on spending Christmas here with my favorite girl."

"You're such a flirt, you know that?" A light shade of pink covers my mum's cheeks.

"That's what the ladies tell me."

We both let out a loud, boisterous laugh. Everything between Meghan and I won't be fixed overnight, but she is my forever and that's all that matters.

Christmas with my mum was just how it used to be when I was younger, filled with lots of love. It would have been better if Meghan had been there with us, but that's my fault. With an extra suitcase full of presents for her, I return home to Danville with a plan to win her back.

My first order of business is to begin preparations for spring semester. My original plans didn't leave much time, but I wanted to spend as much time with Meghan as possible away from Danville.

After heading back to my flat and catching a few hours of sleep, I shower and head directly into the office. Lucky for me, the building is still relatively deserted. No one will be back until after the new year, which means I should be able to get all my work done.

I log in to my school email to find an urgent message from the university's disciplinary committee. I open the email and read.

Dear Dr. Armstrong,

You have been summoned to stand before the Danville University Disciplinary Committee in response to a complaint filed by another faculty member.
We request your presence at a preliminary hearing to discuss it further. Should disciplinary action be

required, a second hearing will be scheduled. You may have a representative from the Danville University Professors' Union present, but it is not required.

Below are the details of the hearing. Please arrive on time, as we will begin promptly at 9:00 a.m. on the day of the hearing.

Sincerely,
Alicia Barnard
Office of Faculty and Student Conduct

There is only one person who could have filed a complaint: Stephanie. Meghan was right all along. I continue reading and notice the date of the hearing is tomorrow, which doesn't give me a lot of time to prepare. No matter. Thankfully, I took Samuel's advice and began compiling my case against Stephanie.

"Enough with the games, Stephanie. You've gone too far, and now it's time for you to pay," I growl into my empty office.

I pull up the hidden files with the information I have on her and hit the print button.

As the pictures and the letters from different faculty members and students print out, I open a

Word document and type up my letter of resignation.

I will not be the reason Meghan doesn't graduate. We may not have parted on the best of terms, but she *will* graduate. I will take care of her because that is what Daddy promised her he would do.

Daddy always keeps his promises.

CHAPTER TWENTY-TWO

MEGHAN

The rest of my winter break is completely miserable. Julian permeated so much of my life, and I didn't realize it until I was forced to sleep in my apartment for the first time in months. Julian and I were practically living together, and now I'm alone in a place that doesn't feel like home.

I bury myself in work, forging ahead on my capstone project, even if Stephanie rejected it. If I'm lucky enough to find another advisor on such short notice, I want to present them with a complete project that is entirely my own. The research is hard and tedious, and I come across more than one article written by Dr. Julian Armstrong, but it distracts me.

It keeps my mind from wandering to what could have been. What should have been.

A week before the new semester starts, I receive an email from Dr. Nelson, agreeing to be my new advisor. I eagerly respond and set up an appointment to meet with him after classes start.

I have a light load this semester. Only three classes, and then I'm done. All requirements should be fulfilled, but I plan on asking Dr. Nelson just to be sure.

Honestly, Dr. Nelson's email and the start of classes lift my spirits. But I'm still more than a little disappointed that Julian hasn't tried to contact me. He has to be back by now.

You are not that girl, I scold myself when I contemplate heading to his apartment. *You are not desperate and needy.*

Oh, who am I kidding? Yes, I am.

Julian fills an emptiness inside me I never knew existed until we met. And now I ache for him every day we're apart.

I'm confident he'll come back, though. We just need a bit of separation to sort out love from lust, reality from fantasy.

On the day of my appointment with Dr. Nelson, I trudge through the cold snow to his office. I stop for a moment and glance down the hallway toward Julian's office. I'm no longer his TA so I don't know his new office hours or schedule.

My watch beeps, and I know I'm late for my meeting with Dr. Nelson. I quickly shake away the fog and hurry in the opposite direction toward his office.

The moment I arrive, it's all business. He asks about my previous project and admits to agreeing with both Stephanie and Julian.

"Ophelia is a very over-done topic," he states. "But I'm very excited to hear what you've come up with regarding Desdemona. There's so much depth there to be explored."

I smile, confident I'll blow him away with my project, and begin explaining. He listens intently and asks questions that will guide me deeper into my research. When we're finished, I'm excited to hurry back to my apartment and finish my work.

"I can't say I'm sorry about your previous advisor."

"Stephanie? Did something happen?"

"She was terminated before the semester started. I'm not sure what happened, but she made a complaint against a member of the faculty, and it blew up in her face."

I sit back in my chair, stunned. Obviously, her complaint was against Julian, but I knew he was keeping tabs on her, compiling all sorts of information should she decide to go after either of us.

"It's a shame about Dr. Armstrong too."

I sit up and my eyes pop open. "What about him?"

"Resigned. He'll finish out the year, but that's it. Such a pity, because Danville could use someone like him on our faculty."

My heart thunders in my chest, and I'm almost positive Dr. Nelson can hear it.

"That is too bad," I murmur.

Dr. Nelson is oblivious to my feelings. We arrange to meet in another month and discuss my project before scheduling my final presentation. Then I'm dismissed.

Automatically, I stand and sling my bag across my shoulder.

Julian resigned. He's going to leave Danville. And me.

The instant I step outside, the floodgates open and I burst into soul-shattering sobs. How could he do this to me? To us?

In a daze, I walk down the hallway, my head

lowered and my eyes blurry. I have no idea where I'm going, nor do I care.

Until I run into a hard wall of muscle with a familiar scent.

"Little one?" Julian's voice is a low rumble.

His hands fold around my arms, holding me steady. But I can't bring myself to look up at him. I reach up and grab his fine wool coat before resting my head against his middle. My body shakes as I continue to cry.

"Come with me," he says, wrapping his arms around me tightly and guiding me down the hall and into his office.

He settles me in a chair across from his desk and kneels in front of me, placing a finger under my chin and guiding it up until we're eye-to-eye.

"Tell me what's wrong."

"You're leaving me," I wail as fresh tears stream steadily down my cheeks.

He clicks his tongue. "Who told you that?"

"Dr. Nelson," I blubber. "I just had a meeting with him, and he said you resigned."

"I did resign. From the university. Not from you, Megs."

His voice is soft and soothing, and soon, my tears dry up.

"But you haven't called me or anything."

He sighs and moves to sit beside me. "I'm sorry, but a lot has happened since I returned to Danville. You were right about Stephanie. She filed a complaint against me, but I was ready for her."

"I figured as much when Dr. Nelson told me Stephanie was gone." My eyes seem to finally open, and I notice the boxes scattered around the office. "You're really leaving Danville?"

"I only came here for one reason. *You.* And if I don't have that, why stay?"

"You can have me, Julian. All of me. *Please.*" I want to get down on my knees and beg him to come back.

"I want that more than anything, little one. I'll come back when I can keep the promises I make." He stands and bends to kiss me softly on the cheek. "I'm meeting a friend for drinks. Stay if you want."

He brushes past me, and I hear the door open and shut. My chest aches, but I cling to his words.

I'll come back when I can keep the promises I make.

Be patient, I tell myself.

Easier said than done.

CHAPTER TWENTY-THREE

JULIAN

I'm a fucking idiot, I repeat in my head as I shut the door behind me and head toward The Horney Toad to grab a pint with Samuel.

He's been having as rough of a go at it as I have. Who knew women were such trouble? Life was easier as a bachelor, but it was fucking lonely. Meghan makes everything worthwhile, but dear Lord, all this *forever* bullshit is painful. Life would be so much easier if it were black and white. I've always found the gray area tricky.

Meghan is mine. End of story.

I want to be with her forever. Who the fuck cares when—or if—we get married or have children? I certainly don't. It'll happen when it happens.

But I know that isn't good enough for Meghan. And if I want her back, she's going to need more.

As I walk across campus toward the pub, my mind wanders back to the disciplinary committee meeting a few weeks ago.

When I opened the door to the conference room, the three committee members all looked up at me with grim expressions, and next to them was Stephanie, looking like a smug cunt.

"Dr. Armstrong, do you have any idea why you have been summoned here today?" the head of the disciplinary committee asked.

"Don't have the foggiest, but I'm forming one or two ideas," I replied as I slowly took my seat across from them.

"Dr. Francis claims you've engaged in inappropriate behavior with one of your students. Is that true, Dr. Armstrong?"

"Yes, it's true," I admitted quietly.

All three members sucked in sharp breaths.

"However, my relationship with Ms. Webb began prior to my employment with Danville University."

I reached into my bag and pulled out the folder

containing all the "evidence" I might need to defend myself.

"Per my contract, I wasn't even supposed to have a TA. However, Dr. Francis broke that contract when she assigned Ms. Webb to me."

Stephanie pouted and batted her eyelashes. "I only have the best interest of my students in mind. Ms. Webb was in danger of not graduating and this was the only solution I could think of. If I had known about this relationship, I would never have assigned her to be your TA."

I bit my tongue because rude things were on the tip of it, ready to trickle out. "On the first day of classes, I approached you and requested Ms. Webb's schedule be changed. Ms. Webb even approached you and made a similar request. You denied us both."

The three members of the committee all looked in Stephanie's direction until one finally spoke.

"Is this true?"

Stephanie's smile faltered. "Of course not."

"Moving along," the head of the committee interjected. "Dr. Francis has also filed a sexual harassment complaint against you. We gave her the option of not being present for this, but she was adamant about confronting you."

I bet she was, *I thought to myself.*

"Gobshite," I spat out. "Whatever claim she made is utter gobshite."

"Dr. Armstrong, this is a very serious accusation."

"I know it is! But if anyone on this campus is guilty of sexual harassment, it's Dr. Francis." I pushed to my feet and slammed identical packets of information in front of all three members. "Here you will find affidavits from fellow faculty and even students about Dr. Francis's inappropriate behavior toward them. She has flirted, propositioned, and even engaged in sexual encounters with several men and women on this campus."

I stepped back and paused for a moment, letting the three members read through the information.

"She also promised many people positions here at Danville or better grades because of said favors. If anyone should be here in front of the committee, it's her."

If looks could kill, I'd have been a dead man. One glance at Stephanie's red face, and I knew I had her.

"Thank you, Dr. Armstrong. You're dismissed."

. . .

A few days ago, I received word my case was dismissed, and Stephanie was immediately terminated. I can't wait to share the news with Samuel. He'll probably want to stop by her office and gloat...or get one more quick fuck before she leaves.

As I approach The Horney Toad, the large wooden front door swings open and two boys from my Intro to Shakespeare class stumble out, barely making it to the curb before one of them pukes.

"Americans need to learn to hold their liquor," I mutter.

I catch the heavy door before it closes and head inside, immediately spotting Samuel at a high-top table tucked into the back corner. It's rather full for it being late afternoon, but it is the start of the semester. The seniors are probably taking a lighter load, preparing for graduation.

"Took your ass long enough, old man." Samuel pushes a glass of scotch across the table, and I catch it before it hits the floor.

"I ran into someone on my way over," I mumble before throwing back my drink and signaling the barkeep for another.

"Is your new little girl not putting out or something?"

A rumbling growl fills my chest.

Samuel leans back with fear in his eyes. "Sorry. I won't bring her up again."

The barkeep brings over my scotch, but I stop him before he leaves.

"Just bring the whole fucking bottle. I'm going to need it."

With a nod of understanding, he turns back toward the bar and returns with the bottle. I splash a healthy pour into my glass, toss it back, and repeat the process.

"Julian, you need to slow down." Samuel reaches out, taking the bottle from my hand. "What the fuck is going on with you? It's like you've lost your mind."

"It feels that way." I can hear my words slur. "She's gone, and it's all my fault. I couldn't promise forever. Not yet, anyway."

"Back the fuck up. Explain yourself."

I tell him everything. He already knew about the business with Stephanie, but not that I took Meghan to meet my mum.

"You took her to meet your *mother*? You've got it bad for this girl!"

"Don't you think I know that? I want to spend the rest of my life with her, Samuel. Truly, I do."

"Yeah, well, you're acting like a giant pussy." He signals the barkeep to the table, telling him something in hushed tones before turning back in my direction.

"From everything you've told me, Meghan adores you. And you feel the same way. So, what's the goddamn problem?"

The bartender appears with a huge pitcher of water and a glass.

"Drink this." Samuel shoves a glass of water in my face before handing the half-empty bottle of scotch and a hundred-dollar bill back to the bartender. "That should cover what he drank from the bottle."

He stands and pulls his jacket off the back of the chair before sliding his arm into it.

"Where the fuck do you think you are going?" After chugging the water, I feel a little less drunk, but I pour myself another to be on the safe side.

"I'm going to find your little one and see if she'd like a new Daddy," he says.

I growl. I know Samuel's testing me, but my fingers tighten around the glass and the alcohol in my system heightens my annoyance.

"Keep your filthy hands away from my little one. She's *mine!* Do you fucking hear me? Friend or not, if you go anywhere near her, I will fucking end you."

"I'd never do that to you, Julian, but if you don't pull your head out of your ass, someone *will* come along and take her away from you. If you want to be with her, then do something about it. I doubt she'll wait around for your sorry ass forever. I wouldn't."

He's right. Meghan shouldn't have to wait until I figure my shit out for us to be together. I've resigned from Danville, and although I can get my position back at Cambridge, is that what I really want?

No. What I want is Meghan.

My little one.

I finish the last of the water, push back from the table, and head out the door. I need to figure out a way to make a promise to her. A promise that, no matter what she decides, I can keep. Because breaking another promise to my little one is not an option.

CHAPTER TWENTY-FOUR

MEGHAN

I don't know what Julian is waiting for, but it's pissing me off.

Amid working on a paper for a course on Biblical women, there's a knock on my door. I set my laptop aside and make my way to the door. Whoever this is better have pizza, because I'm starving.

When I open the door, Julian is standing there, all smoldering and handsome. My breath hitches slightly and my heart stutters. But that's it. My excitement over seeing him is replaced with annoyance.

"Good evening," he says with a slight nod of his head. "Can I come in?"

"Sure," I say, opening my door wider and turning my back.

Julian's large hand latches on to my arm and spins me.

"Don't walk away from me, little one," he purrs before his lips crash down on mine in a hard, hot kiss.

My hands find their way up to his chest and I push myself away, breaking our connection.

"What are you doing here?" I breathe.

"I thought it would be obvious." His eyes follow me as I walk across the room and sit down in the armchair where I was working.

"You can't just show up and expect me to fall into your arms simply because you're no longer afraid of commitment."

He sits down on my old, lumpy sofa and leans back, stretching out his arms over the back. Shit, he looks so fucking delicious. Why the hell am I resisting?

"I'd never expect that, Megs. But I assumed—"

"That I'd be a little happier to see you? I have a lot going on right now. Three papers to write, plus finishing my capstone project. Pardon me if I don't fall at your feet."

The muscle in his jaw tenses and his eyes narrow. "You're walking a fine line here, little one."

I sigh. "Just tell me why you're here."

"Fine. I've spent the last week thinking about our relationship. Now that Stephanie is gone and the disciplinary committee knows about us, we don't need to sneak around."

I open my mouth to reply, but he holds up a hand.

"Let me finish before you lash me with your tongue again. When I tell you you're mine forever, I mean it. I want you by my side, in my bed, in my *life*, until I take my last breath. I want to marry you and eventually start a family, but not yet. All of that will happen in due time. I apologize for not telling you these things sooner, for putting us both through the hell of these last few weeks, especially when deep down, I knew all along what I wanted."

He reaches into his pocket and pulls out a small red box. When he lifts the lid, a sparkling round diamond twinkles up at me.

"Marry me," he says softly.

My heart thunders with excitement. I want to launch myself at him, smother him with kisses, and forgive him for everything, but I've also been doing some thinking of my own.

"I want to say yes, Julian. More than anything. But you need to give me some time."

"How much time do you need, exactly?"

"Enough time to finish this paper on Ruth's submission to God."

He snorts with soft laughter before he takes my hand and slides the gold band down my ring finger.

"I'll see you tonight, then." He pushes to his feet, his large frame eating up the space in my small living room. "When you're finished, come to my flat, ready to resume your role as my little one."

I know the expected response, but I hold it inside for a moment.

"Yes, Daddy," I finally whisper.

I know it's cliché to show up to a man's apartment in a trench coat with nothing on underneath, but Julian will expect me to be ready the moment I arrive. He'll want to devour and consume me without unnecessary barriers.

There is a small twitch of apprehension the moment I raise my hand to knock on his door.

This is it, I remind myself. *There is no going back after tonight.*

When the door swings open, the sight of Julian leaves me breathless. He's wearing a plain white button-down with the sleeves rolled up and the top few buttons undone, revealing a glimpse of his broad, muscled chest and black trousers impeccably tailored to fit him.

"You came," he says with a smile.

"You didn't think I would?"

"A small doubt." He steps aside and motions for me to enter.

When his hands land on my shoulders and tug at my coat, I stop him.

"Aren't you staying?"

Suddenly, I feel embarrassed. Maybe I shouldn't have arrived completely naked under my long, down-filled coat.

"No, I'm staying."

I slowly shrug off my coat until it falls away and I'm standing in front of him, completely bare. His eyes immediately darken, and a low growl rumbles from his lips.

"It seems we both have different expectations," he says as he circles me slowly.

His breath tickles my skin as he runs his nose along the bare ridge of my shoulder, trailing soft kisses along it and up my neck. His hands land on my hips, gripping them firmly as he pulls me back.

He's already hard; I can feel his length pressing against my back.

"What does my little one need?"

"Her daddy," I moan out as one hand slides up my stomach and cups one breast.

He rolls my nipple between his fingers, tugging it to a stiff peak.

"Kneel," he purrs.

I sink to the floor, waiting for him. He comes around to stand in front of me; his nimble fingers unbuckle his belt and unfasten the button of his pants.

"Open," he commands as he pulls his cock free.

I'm ready for him as he places the tip right on the edge of my tongue. His fingers brush along my jaw as he speaks.

"I'm going to fuck your mouth, little one. I'm going to make you gag on my cock, and you will kneel like a good girl and take everything I give you. Do you understand?"

I flutter my lashes and do my best to nod. His smile fills his entire face. His approval means everything to me.

He places his hands on either side of my head and drives himself deep into my mouth, hitting the back of my throat. I breathe through it, trying not to gag, and he holds himself there before pulling back. He jams his cock down my throat repeatedly until my saliva coats it. He slips out and runs the head along my lips.

"I want to come all over your beautiful face," he murmurs. "But I'm going to save it all for your delicious pussy."

He teases my lips open and demands I suck him. I'm happy to oblige. My hands reach up and wrap around the thick shaft, holding him steady while I lick, suck, and tease him. He hisses his appreciation and drives his fingers through my hair, tugging at the strands.

"Fuck, little one," he moans.

I worship him with my mouth and tongue until he stops me.

"No more," he says breathlessly. "Get up."

I rise slowly, letting the blood rush back to my lower half. He directs me to the leather couch and bends me over the arm. The slap across my ass is sharp and unexpected. But it's followed by the stroke of his fingers between my folds.

"You left me," he grits out after another stinging smack. "You had every right to leave, but it still hurt."

"I know," I whisper.

"Don't do it again."

"Never," I moan as his mouth covers my center.

I turn my head to see him on his knees behind me, his hands on my ass spreading the cheeks and his face buried between my legs. His tongue is heavenly as he licks me from front to back, and when he teases my clit with it, I whimper. It feels like forever since we've been together, and my body is quick to explode.

But Julian denies me my release.

"I can't wait anymore," he snarls right before his cock plunges inside me.

He's rough, and my body is uncomfortably bent over the arm of the couch, but I don't care and neither does he. His grip on my hips is firm and almost painful, but we both need this. We both need the harshness of reconnecting. He needs to own my body and I need to submit to his desires.

"Daddy," I gasp.

"That's right," he grits out. "I'm your fucking daddy, little one."

He drives his cock deep into me with a ferocious sound. His cock pulses inside me as he fills me with his first orgasm.

The light kisses along my back are a sharp contrast to the feral way he used me, but they are a sign of love. A gift for trusting him to use my body as he pleased.

"I love you." His words are whispered against my skin. "And I'm going to love you every day for the rest of my life."

EPILOGUE
JULIAN

Three months later

"**M**egs," I call down the hall. "Darling, I've got to meet up with the rest of the faculty."

There's a stack of mail sitting on the counter that needs sorting before we leave tomorrow. One envelope in particular catches my eye. I pluck it from the stack and see Meghan's name printed neatly.

She steps out of the bedroom, messing with her hair. She looks bloody gorgeous. Her blonde hair cascades around her face in golden waves and her blue eyes sparkle with excitement.

"Okay," she says as she fusses with an earring. "I'll see you after the ceremony."

"What's this?" I hold up the piece of mail.

"A letter from Oxford," she says nonchalantly.

"Clearly, little one. But I thought we agreed you were going to apply to Cambridge for grad school."

"I was going to…" Her voice trails off as she looks around the room.

"But?"

Her lips thin into a tight smile. "But I really want to study under Dr. Montrose."

"I live in Cambridge, Meghan. How is this supposed to work if you live two and a half hours away?"

"Dr. Montrose said there's an opening for you, if you want it."

I scoff. "I will not give up my tenure at Cambridge for a subpar position at a subpar university. You'll just have to tell Dr. Montrose you've changed your mind."

"You're kidding, right? Julian, I won't give up on my dreams simply because you're too snobbish and stubborn."

My mouth drops and my fingers twitch. "I

should take you over my knee right this second, little one."

"But you won't, 'cause I'm right."

Admittedly, she *is* correct. It is unfair of me to ask her to give up on something she's wanted for years.

"Fine. I guess I can rent a flat in Oxford and make the drive. I'll have to get you a car as well."

"You don't have to do that," she says, holding up a hand. "I've already applied for graduate accommodations. I want to live on campus."

"Christ, Meghan. We're engaged to be married, but you're planning a life without me! When were you planning on telling me this?"

Her eyes dart around the room. "I didn't think it would be a problem, Julian. I'm sorry."

I pinch the bridge of my nose. "If we don't leave now, we're going to be late." I look up at her, pinning her with my gaze. "But don't think we're finished discussing this."

"Okay," she says with a nod.

And because I'm a total goner when it comes to my little one, I pull her against me.

"I'm so proud of you, little one," I whisper, letting my fingers dance along the hem of her dress before skimming them up her thighs and teasing them across her bare pussy.

I growl with approval. Damn, I want to fuck her! I've kept my hands to myself during these last few weeks because we've both been extremely busy. Even after Meghan successfully presented and defended her capstone project to an intimidating trio of professors, I remained a saint.

I retreat, removing my hand. "If we both didn't have someplace to be right now, your pretty pink dress would be in a pretty pink pile, and you'd be impaled on my cock." I lean forward and brush my lips against hers. "I'll see you after the ceremony."

I leave before I change my mind. Instead, I focus on the immediate future.

Tomorrow, we're going on a holiday redo. Part of Meghan's graduation gift is a week in Cornwall, at a luxury resort right on Carne Beach, though I doubt we'll see much of anything beyond the four walls of our room.

I suffer through the pomp and circumstance of Danville's graduation ceremony for Meghan. The doctoral robes are heavy and hot, and the hood practically strangles me, but the moment her name is called, pride swells in my chest. I nearly forget all about her acceptance to Oxford.

When she walks up on the stage, I break protocol and stand. She glances in my direction and smiles shyly. Her cheeks are red with embarrassment, but I don't really give a fuck. She's mine and while I take great pleasure from her body, her mind is quite spectacular.

"Finally," I murmur to my neighbor at the ceremony's conclusion.

He nods, and we stand before exiting the dais in a single-file line.

Everyone is gathered in the auditorium's main entrance, and I scramble to find Meghan in a sea of families, professors, and graduates. I find her in the middle of the chaos, chatting happily with a small group of classmates. I push through the crowd to get to her and when I do, propriety be damned.

"I'm so fucking proud of you," I tell her with a single breath before gathering her in my arms and kissing her hard.

She's tense, but I'm persistent, teasing her lips open with my tongue until she relaxes against me. My hand slides up her back and tangles in her long blonde waves as our kiss deepens. She moans into my kiss, but I feel her hand press against my chest and reluctantly, we part.

Her blue eyes are filled with surprise as she looks around at the people, gaping.

"Julian," she whispers. "What do you think you're doing?"

"Kissing you," I state matter-of-factly.

"Clearly! Everyone saw you!"

"Who cares! You've graduated. What are they going to do, take away your degree?"

The flush on her cheeks deepens, and I brush my fingers along her jaw.

"I love you, Meghan." I kiss her again, softer this time, and she melts against me with a sigh. "Now, let's get out of here. We've got a mess to sort out."

The crowd in the auditorium's lobby has thinned, making our escape easier. Thankfully, no one bothers to stop either of us as we head toward the exit. The campus is small, so it doesn't take long to return home. The moment we step through the front door, I pin Meghan against it.

"If you want to go to Oxford, fine. Go to Oxford," I grit out.

One hand travels the length of her body and roughly palms her breast.

"But *we* are not living together in ancient campus housing. I don't care if you get into Magdalen College. I refuse to live in a tiny room with you."

She moans as I suck at the delicate skin on her neck.

"I did," she says breathlessly. "Get into Magdalen College."

Pride swells inside me. "Of course, you did, little one. You're bloody brilliant."

We're both still wearing our ridiculous graduation robes, and I grasp the tiny zipper of hers between my fingers and tug it down.

"But that doesn't mean I'm living there. We'll find someplace in town." My fingers make their way under her dress, but she stops me.

"What did you mean when you said we aren't living together on campus?"

I step back and blink. "I sent Dr. Montrose a text before the start of the ceremony, accepting her offer."

"Julian!" Her voice is a high-pitched screech which nearly renders me deaf.

But it's her smile that guts me. It lights up her beautiful face. I'm a lucky fucking man because she is going to be my wife. She throws herself at me, nearly knocking me over, and I laugh at her exuberance.

"Come on, little one," I purr into her ear as I drag her toward the bedroom. "Daddy wants to celebrate properly."

Thank you for reading Daddy's Little One from Myself! I hope you loved Julian and Meghan's story. If you did, or even if you didn't, I would be so grateful if you could please leave a review.

The Scandalous Daddies Series continues with Samuel and Avery's story in Daddy's Dirty Girl. To learn more or grab a copy just click the title!

USA Today Bestselling Author AJ Alexander is a wannabe psychologist who writes short, sweet, and steamy age gap romances about blue collar men and the girls that love them!

She's a cynical hopeless romantic that believes in love at first sight, that bigger is always better, and everything should be put off for a nap.

https://www.authorajalexander.com/books

- amazon.com/author/ajalexander
- bookbub.com/authors/aj-alexander
- facebook.com/AJAlexanderAuthor
- goodreads.com/authorajalexander
- instagram.com/ajalexanderauthor

Made in the USA
Middletown, DE
26 July 2022

70051311R00111